THE FOURTH SHADOW

Simon Larren merely had to ensure that the visiting President of Maraquilla remained alive during a goodwill tour of the British Crown Colony of San Quito. But there were complications. Maraquilla's President could no longer trust his regular bodyguard, and Larren was hampered by Caroline Brand, the good-time girl who had followed him from London. And finally there was a Communist-inspired bid for illegal independence from British rule, backed by the evil of voodoo.

ROBERT CHARLES

THE FOURTH SHADOW

Complete and Unabridged

LINFORD
Leicester

First published in Great Britain in 1966

First Linford Edition
published 1997

British Library CIP Data

Charles, Robert, *1938*—
    The fourth shadow.—Large print ed.—
    Linford mystery library
    1. Detective and mystery stories
    2. Large type books
    I. Title
    823.9'14 [F]

    ISBN 0–7089–5064–7

Published by
F. A. Thorpe (Publishing) Ltd.
Anstey, Leicestershire

Set by Words & Graphics Ltd.
Anstey, Leicestershire
Printed and bound in Great Britain by
T. J. Press (Padstow) Ltd., Padstow, Cornwall

This book is printed on acid-free paper

1

Caribbean Assignment

SIMON LARREN watched impassionately as the giant VC1O airliner roared slowly to a halt. It was night, but the sleek silver shape gleamed brightly in the blaze of light thrown from the ever-busy passenger building at London Airport. A few moments later a clear female voice announced the imminent departure of Flight No. 375 for Bermuda, Aparicio and Miami, and Larren moved slowly to join the cluster of passengers assembling around the air hostess who would shepherd them aboard the waiting plane.

As always he wondered whether this flight — this assignment — was to be his last.

There was no reason why it should

be. The job was outside his normal sphere, but technically it was straightforward and simple; at least, as simple as any job could ever be in his business. But even so, at the very beginning, there was always this brief moment of doubt.

His fellow-passengers were moving out towards the plane, following the lead of the pretty hostess, and Larren fell into step beside them. As he walked he pondered on how remarkably little he really knew of the organization of which he was part. He knew very few of its personnel, and practically nothing of its range on influence and intrigue in which he was not directly involved. He knew why of course. He was a lone operator: a killer who preferred the direct clash of conflict with the enemy in the field. He was not the mould of agent who could be groomed for an administrative post, or for any kind of permanent undercover position, and so it was not necessary for him to know too much. In fact it was best that he knew as little as possible, for the assignments to which his capabilities best fitted were the violent ones that carried the biggest risks. And it was a proven fact that even the most loyal and trusted agent could be made to talk under modern methods of torture.

He realized that his thoughts were fast becoming morbid again, and deliberately changed them. He found his seat in the airliner, ordered a large scotch to be served the moment they were in the air, and then sat back and mentally reviewed his briefing for the job in hand.

His destination was Aparicio, the capital city of the British Crown Colony of San Quito, a single large island in the Caribbean sea. Like most of the remaining fragments of the British Empire San Quito was almost ready for independence and already had its own Parliament, headed by their President and leader of the People's Progressive Party, a man named Vicente Dominguez. At the moment Dominguez was proposing to entertain President Jose Rafael of the Central American state of Maraquilla for a six-day tour and goodwill visit to the Colony, and that was where Simon Larren came in.

He had listened carefully as the little man who called himself simply Mr Smith had explained the facts in the Whitehall office. Then he said bluntly.

"You don't sound very happy about it?"

"No," Smith had retorted. "And a lot of people on San Quito aren't happy about it either. Jose Rafael is a dictator, and the people of San Quito don't relish the idea of their Government extending hospitality to the man. Besides which there's a Communist movement on the island which has been clamouring for full independence for some time, mainly because they feel that they can wrest power from Dominguez once he loses full British backing. There's a possibility that they'll use Rafael's visit to stir up as much trouble as they can."

Larren frowned. "If those are the circumstances, then why is Dominguez creating trouble for himself by staging this goodwill tour? What's the point?"

"The answer to that is that Dominguez suffers from the same blind fault as a score of other leaders of minor countries and states. He believes himself destined to play a guiding role in world politics. He has a praise-worthy, but unworkable idea for stabilizing the whole Caribbean area. He believes that he can do it by inviting the leaders of all the countries around him to visit San Quito in turn, and at the same time persuading them to extend invitations to each other. In short he wants to start a chain reaction of these goodwill tours to generate trust and friendship, and, I suppose, to set an example to the rest of the world. He sees himself as some kind of saviour, contributing to peace where other world leaders have failed. He's a brilliant orator, and has the full support of his cabinet."

"But why start with Maraquilla and Rafael?" Larren persisted.

"Because the larger countries would probably ignore him. He has to start with the smaller, unimportant countries who will be impressed by his invitation and his ideas. Once he's got a few of those to respond and staged some successful tours then he's in a better position to make the bigger countries take notice."

Larren made a sardonic smile. "And I suppose Maraquilla is the smallest place there is?"

"It's pretty near," Smith agreed. "It's the smallest country in Central America anyway, and of course Central America comes within Dominguez's vision of the Caribbean sphere. There is also the fact that Rafael has a vain streak which made it practically certain that he would accept the first invitation."

"So Dominguez is willing to disrupt his own country in order to play at peace leader before the world?"

Smith gave it a moment's thought. "I'd say that was unfair to Dominguez," he said at last. "His intentions are basically good, and I don't think he anticipated such a violent reaction in San Quito. Most of it has been deliberately stirred up by the Communists, and although he should have foreseen such a development I don't believe that he did. Now he's in a position where he can't cancel Rafael's visit without collapsing his whole plan and losing a lot of face, and he won't do that."

Larren frowned. "But what about the British Governor on San Quito, surely he must have a say in the island's administration? It is still a British Crown Colony."

Smith shook his head wearily. "Normally that's true. But San Quito is nearing independence, and that puts Sir Basil Trafford in a delicate spot. Theoretically he still has authority, but he must apply it tactfully if we are to retain the island's goodwill after he leaves. He must take more and more of a back seat until he ultimately hands over control altogether. Naturally Sir Basil will take emergency measures if they become necessary, but they must he really necessary before he can act. He has advised Dominguez to stop Rafael's visit, but Dominguez insists that if he backs down then he will lose the faith of his supporters. And so the tour will go on."

"An awkward situation," Larren observed. "But where do I fit in?"

Smith said bluntly. "You fit in because it would harm British prestige if Jose Rafael were to be assassinated while touring one of our colonies, especially as such an event could be exploited and cause major trouble on the island itself. Normally Rafael would rely on his own bodyguard to protect him. He has three regular shadows, all hand-picked killers. But unfortunately he can no longer trust those three men. He believes that one of them may have sold out to his enemies, the rival factions back home in Maraquilla."

Smith's pudgy face was serious as he went on. "There have been two recent attempts on Rafael's life in Maraquilla. The first during a visit he made to inspect one of his army posts. A land mine blew up the car directly in front of the one in which he was travelling and killed four of his staff officers. The trip was supposed to be a secret and so its fairly obvious that someone close to him must have betrayed his movements.

"Shortly afterwards there was an attempt to poison him. Rafael noticed a slight discoloration in the wine he was about to drink, but one of his bodyguards, an American named Hansen, saw it at the same time and smashed the glass from Rafael's hand. That could either clear Hansen, or it could mean that he was watching more closely because he knew the wine was poisoned. He could have made a show to divert suspicion when he saw that Rafael was not going to drink. In any case, Rafael is no longer sure of his bodyguards, and as it is in British interests to see that he stays alive while on San Quito at least, I've been ordered to provide him with a fourth bodyguard for the duration of his visit."

Smith paused, his deep grey eyes fixed on Larren's face. Very few people would have credited Smith with his controlling position in Counter-espionage, but those who knew could look into those eyes and believe.

He went on. "Rafael is very happy to have a fourth shadow, but I don't expect that his present bodyguard will be so friendly. And if one of them is a traitor then he might even feel that a new arrival will be best out of the way. That's why the man I send has to be another seasoned killer — someone who can hold his own against experts. And it's for the rare job like this that I need to keep you around."

Larren had smiled wryly. "I am getting stale," he admitted. "I think I'll enjoy some Caribbean sunshine."

2

Night Flight to Aparicio

LARREN was still musing over the details of his mission as the last, late-arriving passengers filed into the airliner, and he did not notice as one of them made directly for the vacant seat beside him. The delighted sound of her voice startled him as it swirled gaily into his thoughts.

"Simon! How lovely. Don't tell me that you're going to San Quito too. I had hoped that you might be, but I didn't really expect it to come true!"

Her presence was so unexpected that for a moment he could only stare. She stood there in a light pink travelling costume, holding a matching handbag and a B.O.A.C. zip bag in one white-gloved hand. A leather camera case hung from one shoulder and a perky little red hat was balanced on her dark gold hair, its whisp of pink lace lying prettily on her forehead. She was smiling, and looking down at him as though she too couldn't quite believe her bright blue eyes.

Her name was Caroline Brand, and the last time he had seen her had been the previous night, when he had slept with her after explaining that he would be out of town for a while. She had been the only private affair that had needed tidying up between his briefing and boarding the plane, and up till this moment he had already forgotten her.

"Caroline!" he said at last. "What the devil — ?"

She smiled happily and sat down beside him.

"Isn't this a wonderful coincidence, Simon! I've been trying all day to contact you and let you know. I phoned your flat in Rushlake Terrace five times but there was no answer, and so I thought that you must have already left on an earlier plane. You know, you didn't say exactly where you were going in the Caribbean on your silly business trip, or which flight you would be on."

She paused suddenly. "Are you going to San Quito, too, Simon? Or — " Her voice became doubtful. " — or perhaps you're getting off at Bermuda?"

Larren had controlled his first shock of surprise, and now he smiled at her quizzically. It was impossible to deny his destination if she was to accompany him all the way, and so he spoke frankly.

"As it happens I am going to San Quito, the business that my firm wants me to handle is in Aparicio."

As he spoke he mentally re-assessed his position. Ostensibly he was employed by the city offices of Clark and Mathews, one of London's largest import and export firms, and at the moment he was supposedly handling a tricky export deal on their behalf. It was a simple but adequate explanation to cover his absence from London,

13

and would stand up to any amount of investigation from that end. Anyone who enquired would learn that a Mr Simon Larren was indeed on that firm's list of top salesmen, and that he was employed on the firm's business in the Caribbean. But unfortunately, on this trip, he could only be covered from the home end, for the very nature of the job meant that he would have to operate practically openly on San Quito. And the presence of a girl who knew him from London made things decidedly awkward.

However, he continued to smile, and said warmly.

"But what are you doing here? What's this wonderful coincidence that you spoke of?"

"It's simple, darling. Tommy Jackson is sick — he's caught some peculiar tropical bug — so I've been sent out to Aparicio to take his place." She saw the blank look that appeared on Larren's face and hastened to clarify the explanation. "Tommy is the news photographer who was sent out with one of our top foreign correspondents to report the story of this state visit by Maraquilla's President. But Tommy's caught this bug quite suddenly, and I'm the only photographer on the *London Mail* who isn't fully weighed down with other commitments. So, my dear old foreign editor, bless his little ink-stained heart, has had no choice but to send me. Naturally, I just jumped at the chance."

She was fumbling with her safety belt as she spoke, and he leaned forward obligingly to slide the buckle tight around her slim waist. The action was casual, and even his eyes showed nothing of his thoughts as he said.

"Well, it certainly is a surprise. I wouldn't have thought it possible."

She laughed. "It's a surprise for me too. And if only I had known last night it would have saved me from being so miserable after you had slaked your appetite and left — you beast!" She smiled at him fondly, and added. "But

I had no idea that this was coming my way until I walked into the office first thing this morning. Isn't it a marvellous stroke of luck?"

"Extraordinary," Larren agreed. The VC10 was moving away from the passenger buildings now and gathering momentum as she sped down the runway, but Larren barely noticed as he watched Caroline Brand's deep blue eyes.

He went on blandly. "But when you first told me that you were a photographer for the *London Mail* I rather presumed that you took pictures of fashions or something. You didn't seem the type to handle the globe-trotting assignments."

Caroline gave him a sad look. "Simon, you're naive. Can you imagine all those sweet young models allowing another woman to paw them around, and tell them how to stand and what to do. They'd hate it. They'll allow a man to do it and enjoy it, but not another woman. No, Simon, we camera girls have to earn our bread and butter the hard way."

The airliner was climbing steeply now, with the airport lights dropping away fast beneath them. They were both silent as they waited for the plane to level out, and Larren's brain was ticking over swiftly.

Caroline's presence on San Quito would have posed unwanted complications in any case, but to have her actually following Rafael's progress with a camera was even worse. She could not fail to notice him in the President's wake, and then she would ask questions. And besides, it was altogether too dubious a coincidence.

He cast his mind back to a West End nightclub, and the circumstances of their first meeting five weeks previously. She had been dining with two friends, a young couple whom she had later explained worked with her on the staff of the *London Mail*. When the young couple had left her alone to dance Larren had crossed to her table and suggested that they follow their example. It had developed from there.

Now he realized that the nightclub had been one which he used frequently, and that Caroline Brand could have been a plant. But planted by whom? And for what purpose?

He admitted that it was possible, and yet it seemed too improbable to believe. And when he thought about it again even the coincidence of her presence aboard this plane was just within the realms of possibility. Her happy smile was too genuine for an amateur, and the whole set-up too amateurish for a professional. Either way it was a damned nuisance.

Then Caroline glanced across at his face and said pointedly.

"Simon, don't look so serious, or I shall begin to think that you don't welcome my company after all."

Larren turned his face towards her and allowed his mouth to relax, his hand resting lightly for a moment on her knee.

"After last night, how could I possibly be so ungallant?"

If he had been her first lover she might have blushed, instead she gave him a quick smile.

"Don't worry, Simon. I know what you're thinking. You're afraid that I'll get in the way of those terribly important export deals you've got to arrange. But you needn't let it bother you because I won't. I'm going to be pretty busy myself for the next six days, otherwise my editor will want to know why."

But then she covered his hand on her knee with her own and added candidly.

"But if you do happen to get a free evening you can always call and see how busy I am. I shall be staying at the Key West Hotel."

★ ★ ★

Just over five hours later, after a brief touchdown at Bermuda, the VC10

19

landed at Aparicio airport on the British Crown Colony of San Quito. By then Caroline Brand was dozing in her seat, and Simon Larren had still not made up his mind whether she was genuine or not.

They separated in the airport terminal, where he made the excuse that he had to telephone his business associates, and that as they were booked into different hotels there was little point in her waiting for him. She accepted that, reminded him of where she was staying and kissed him lightly before she turned away. Larren watched her for a moment and then turned to look for a telephone booth. He did in fact have a long call to make, but not to anyone in San Quito — his call was to London.

He addressed the man who answered as Harry, although it was doubtful if this was the man's real name. He assured this person that he had enjoyed his flight, and even met an old friend — Caroline Brand of the *London Mail*.

Surely Harry remembered her? He rambled on inconsequentially for a few more moments and then hung up.

He was satisfied. If he had addressed the man at the other end of the line as John it would have meant that he had definitely identified Caroline Brand as a hostile agent. If he had addressed the man as Stephen it would have meant that he wanted her removed. There were other variations, but by addressing the man as Harry he had conveyed that he was unsure and wanted a double security check on her background. It was now only a matter of time before he got it.

He left the phone booth and started to walk towards the terminal exit, and then abruptly a voice spoke his name.

"Mr Larren?"

Larren turned as the speaker came up to him. He was a well groomed young man with very fair hair. His cheeks were youthfully smooth but his smile was even and confident. He wore a dark grey double-breasted suit, and a

21

red and grey striped tie that made him as English as roast beef or Trafalgar Square.

He said briskly. "I seem to have missed you as you came through customs. I'm sorry about that. I was supposed to smooth the way. I'm Davison from the Governor's staff." He paused and added. "I'm presuming that you are Mr Simon Larren?"

Larren nodded and produced his passport.

"That's fine." Davison smiled warmly. "I would have felt such a fool if I'd picked up the wrong man." He glanced at the overcoat and the small suitcase that Larren was now carrying, and added. "I'll take one of those if you like. I've got a car waiting for you outside the airport. I know it's still the middle of the night, but Rafael's due here at noon tomorrow and His Excellency wants to see you personally before he arrives. I'm to take you straight to Government House."

Larren made a gesture of assent and

allowed the young man to lead the way. Outside the airport a large highly-polished Daimler saloon was waiting, with a Union Jack curling from its sleek black bonnet. A coloured driver in smart chauffeur's uniform was standing by the door.

Larren preceded Davison into the car, and a few moments later it pulled away smoothly from the airport. It was a warm night and the car's windows were open, allowing a cool indraught of flower-scented air. The graceful palms lining Aparicio's streets showed up clearly in moon and starlight. Davison chatted amiably, saying a lot yet saying nothing.

The car turned away from the centre of the city, heading uphill towards a more expensive residential area. The road was good and the skyline was still splashed with the silhouette of palms, and now with fine, smart villas. Larren was outwardly serene, but now he stilled the warning inner sense that was always alert in any new circumstances.

He knew from the street plans of Aparicio that he had studied before he left London that the Daimler was in fact heading for Government House.

Ten minutes later the Daimler stopped outside the Governor's residence. It was mansionesque, with a white-pillared façade that had remained relatively unchanged since the late seventeenth century when the first British colonists had wrested the island of San Quito from the hands of Spain. It had served as the seat of government ever since, and although renovated several times still retained its original style.

Davison dismissed their driver, and the Daimler swished softly away along the gravel approach as he led Larren on to the grand verandah. There were no sentries here, although there had been at the gates where the Daimler had been forced to stop. Instead there was only a manservant who smiled at Davison in recognition and allowed them in.

"This way," said Davison, and his

voice had lowered to suit the hushed interior of the great hall. Larren followed the young man along a soft red carpet that suitably muffled their footsteps.

Davison stopped at a side door and opened it, and Larren's warning inner sense was fast asleep as he stepped inside. It was an ante room, and it was empty, and only then did Larren start to suspect. The door closed behind him and he turned slowly, knowing that it was too late to hurry.

Davison was standing with his back to the closed door and looking sadly apologetic behind the capably held automatic in his right hand.

He said seriously. "I'm awfully sorry about this, Larren. But would you mind removing your shirt and jacket?"

3

Company of Killers

LARREN remained perfectly still, his grey-green eyes carefully and coldly studying the other man's face. The complete silence of the great hushed house was now distinctly ominous, and Larren could feel each separate beat of his own heart. Davison's smooth face looked just a little pansyish, but despite that the chances of jumping him and getting away with it were exactly nil. At last Larren said calmly.

"It's a strange request."

"It is, isn't it." Davison smiled warmly. "But I assure you it is justified. And it won't take a moment."

Larren shrugged helplessly, then laid his overcoat on the floor and started to remove his tie. His fingers were within three inches of the flat hilt of the razor-edged knife that was reached through the inside pocket of his jacket, but he decided against attempting to reach it. He could flick the knife into Davison's throat, but not before Davison's bullet kicked a hole through his kidneys, and that sort of thing wasn't going to help. He dropped the necktie on his coat and began to take off his jacket.

Davison said seriously. "Perhaps you'd better step back a pace. I'm only an amateur at this, and if I thought you were going to throw that at me I might get nervous and shoot."

Larren smiled thinly, but he obeyed just the same. He dropped the jacket on the floor and then peeled off his shirt. With his arms at his sides he waited.

Davison moved a little closer, his eyes narrowing as he examined Larren's physique.

"Would you lift your left arm?" he asked.

The request had Larren fully baffled, but slowly he raised his arm.

Davison beamed. "A bullet scar across the left ribs," he observed with satisfaction. "And a matching scar across the underside of the left bicep. Plus a nasty knife scar across the back of the right wrist. That's exactly what I hoped I would see."

He lowered the gun and continued cheerfully. "There should be a lower bullet scar nearer the abdominal area, and an old wartime relic above the left ankle, but I think we can take those as proved." He put the gun in his jacket pocket and moved forward to pick up Larren's shirt. As he held it out he went on.

"As I said before, I'm awfully sorry about that. But you were missing for almost fifteen minutes between the time the main bulk of passengers disembarked from your plane and the moment that I found you. That's time enough for one man to be spirited away and for another with a fake passport to be substituted in his place. And there are elements on this island who might just be prepared to go to such lengths."

Larren accepted his shirt. "I had to put a call through to London," he explained. "It takes time to make a connection."

"That's reasonable," Davison admitted. "But if there had been a substitute he would obviously have been provided with a similar explanation to account for the time lapse, so I had to be sure. We had a full description of you from London, but your scars were the one thing it would be impossible to duplicate at short notice. And it would be an awful blunder if we put in the wrong man to shadow Rafael."

Larren dressed calmly and said. "Who are these elements you spoke of?"

"The Communists: They've been making trouble for a long time. Their main aim seems to be to embarrass Dominguez's government, and to play on anything that might bring him into disfavour. There were some minor riots today to protest against this coming tour by Rafael. We're pretty sure that they inspired those."

Larren frowned. "Do you really think that the Communists are well enough organized to have kidnapped me at the airport and planted their own man in my place?"

Davison hesitated. "That's my opinion."

Larren noted the moment of hesitation and said bluntly. "But not Sir Basil Trafford's, or anyone else in authority, is that it?"

Davison was embarrassed. "I'm afraid so," he admitted. "No doubt I shall come in for a heavy rollicking over these last few minutes. I did rather exceed my duty."

Larren gave him a hard look. "Forget it," he said at last. He straightened his tie and added. "Perhaps you'd better take me to Sir Basil. That's if His Excellency did send for me?"

Davison stiffened, and then he turned

to the door. "Sir Basil is waiting," he said flatly.

The younger man's shoulders were firmly squared as he led Larren down to the far end of the great hall. He knocked lightly on the large, elaborately carved door, beneath which the soft red carpet still continued, and then opened it to announce Larren to the answering voice.

The room was large and comfortable. A polished table desk stood by the drawn drapes that shielded the window, and behind it a portrait of Her Majesty The Queen smiled down. The chair behind the desk was empty, and the three occupants of the room were relaxing in large red leather armchairs. There was a faint haze of cigar smoke and the scent of sherry. A large, grey-haired man with an accurately clipped moustache rose from the centre armchair, and Larren knew from the clear blue eyes and slow manner that this was His Excellency Sir Basil Trafford, Her Britannic Majesty's

Governor to San Quito.

"Ah, Mr Larren, welcome to Aparicio." Trafford's hand-shake was slow but firm, exactly as Larren had expected that it would be. "I don't think I need to introduce myself, but the gentleman on your left is Mr Carleton, my Deputy Governor, while the gentleman on your right is Mr Mackenzie, our able but anti-sassenach Commissioner of Police."

Larren shook hands with each man in turn. Carleton was stiff and precise, and there was a tired look in his eyes, as though he rather than Trafford was bearing full responsibility. Mackenzie was heavy with solid features and a crooked smile, and it was he who smoked the cigar.

Davison moved a fourth chair into position and Larren relaxed as Trafford invited him to name his drink. Larren chose Haig and Davison provided it from a large cut glass tray of bottles that stood on a side table. Then Trafford became business-like. He said bluntly.

"I don't know how much you were told before you left London, Larren. But in any case there have been some new developments in the past few hours. I thought it best to bring you up to date."

Larren said calmly. "What kind of new developments?"

"Basically an unconfirmed report that a boat-load of Rafael's enemies from Maraquilla have been landed somewhere on San Quito. Rafael's chief rival back home is an ex-army general named Savalas, and we believe it's possible that Savalas was on that boat. We know that the General has vanished from Maraquilla, and if the report is true then it's most likely that he's involved."

Larren began to sense that the Governor was more worried than he was prepared to reveal on the surface. He said slowly.

"Where did this report originate? And where is the boat supposed to have landed?"

33

Mackenzie answered. "The report seems to have come from the back streets of Aparicio, or from the villages outside the city, from the poorer coloured quarters in fact. I've had some of my best men trying to substantiate the rumours, but either nobody knows for sure, or nobody wants to talk to the police. It's as though the story is being deliberately spread to the people — but there it stops. And if there was a boat it could have landed practically anywhere along the island's coastline, and its occupants could have vanished into the jungle in a matter of moments."

"But what's the purpose?" Larren asked. "What can Savalas hope to achieve here that he couldn't manage equally well in Maraquilla, where he obviously must have some element of support?"

Mackenzie hesitated, and then Trafford answered.

"We're not sure. But at the moment Savalas could have just as much support here as in Maraquilla. If our President Dominguez has any kind of success with his peace plans for the Caribbean, then it's obviously going to set him firmly in the saddle for a long rule after independence. His enemies don't want that, and the best way to sabotage these good-will tours is for the first one to end with the assassination of Rafael. So you can see that Savalas may well have made a temporary alliance with the anti-Dominguez factions here on San Quito. The prospect is quite a headache."

Larren grimaced. "What are the security arrangements for Rafael's visit?"

Trafford said. "Those are in Mackenzie's hands." He looked at the Police Commissioner as he spoke. Mackenzie laid down his cigar and spoke calmly. "The security arrangements are as tight as I can make them. While he's here Rafael will stay at the villa Marola, which is just outside Aparicio. We can guard it more effectively than a hotel, which we would have to clear of all other guests to be one hundred per cent safe. The dangerous moments will be during the day when he'll be attending the various functions that have been laid on for his visit. The route and all the stops will be well guarded by my men of course, and I've got a permanent bodyguard who will be shadowing our own Dominguez. Rafael has his own three shadows, but I'm damned glad that you'll be with them. It's a help to know that there's one man at least on the job that we can wholly trust."

Mackenzie picked up his cigar again and Trafford carried on in his place.

"I think you can safely disregard the outside threats, Larren. Those are Mackenzie's responsibility, and it's no good any one man trying to do too much. If you will concentrate on forestalling any assassination from inside Rafael's own party, then I shall be satisfied. But we feel that it is best if you are acquainted with all the risks."

Larren nodded. "I understand, but

one thing I still don't understand is why you don't step in and stop the whole thing. Surely now that you have reason to believe Savalas is on San Quito you must have enough justification to call it off. Davison mentioned something about riots having taken place already."

Trafford hesitated for a moment, and then attempted to explain. "First the riots, Larren, so far they've been just local disturbances, fired we believe by the Communists, but they haven't been too difficult to handle. As for calling it off, that is difficult. If I force Dominguez to back down, he loses both face and faith with the country. And it is in the interests of Great Britain that that should not happen. Dominguez is in full support of our policies, and the biggest part of my job now is to ensure that he remains in control after we hand over independence." He closed one fist in a sharp gesture to emphasize his point and finished. "At this stage I have to support Dominguez. If I don't this fiasco could finish him."

There was silence, and Larren saw that the Governor was right. Vicente Dominguez had quite simply bitten off more than he could chew, and had realized it too late. And now, to save the President of San Quito's career, and so ensure a future government friendly to Britain, Trafford had to allow Rafael's visit to continue, and ensure that it passed off smoothly. As with every other crisis in the world there was a point of no return where only face was important. Here on San Quito the situation had passed it.

Larren sighed, and then drank the whisky that had so far remained untouched in the glass in his hand. He had the unhappy feeling that he was sitting on a powder barrel with a score of burning fuses. It was inevitable that the barrel must explode, and the only question was in which fuse would burn down first to ignite it.

* * *

It was noon the following day when Jose Rafael's plane landed at Aparicio airport. Larren stood in the background with Davison as Sir Basil Trafford waited with Carleton to receive Maraquilla's President. With the Governor and his Deputy was Vicente Dominguez.

Larren regarded with interest this tall scholarly man whose well-intentioned ideals had prompted the chaos that now threatened to backfire all around him. Dominguez was bare-headed and wore a dark, sober, single-breasted suit that clashed strongly with Sir Basil Trafford's plumed helmet, ceremonial sword and fine white uniform. The president wore dark glasses against the strong sunlight that reflected from the dusty airfield, but seemed perfectly composed as he waited in the heat.

Rafael's private plane, a six-seater business aircraft with the brilliant national colours of Maraquilla painted on her gleaming fuselage, landed exactly on time. A low gangway was swiftly rushed into place and Larren watched as Rafael himself appeared in the opened doorway.

The dictator of Maraquilla wore a light, biscuit coloured suit with a cream shirt and a plain yellow bow tie. His lean, dark-skinned face was shadowed beneath a white panama hat. A gold ring caught the sunlight on his right hand, and a gold wristwatch showed on his left wrist. The whole impression Larren decided, was vulgar.

Dominguez and Trafford moved forward as Rafael descended the gangway, and camera's flashed to cover the brief moments of smiles and handshakes as they met. Larren scanned the faces of the press representatives briefly, but saw no sign of Caroline Brand.

Then Davison touched his arm and said.

"There'll be a luncheon reception at Government House next. He should be pretty safe there. After that he'll be shown his quarters at the villa Marola. That's where you'll merge into his staff. We may as well have a meal ourselves, and then get over to the villa before he arrives." He smiled lamely and added. "I owe you a lunch for not complaining to the Governor last night."

* * *

It was three hours later before Larren faced the man whose footsteps he was to shadow for the next five days. He had fully explored the villa Marola while waiting Rafael's arrival, and was satisfied with Mackenzie's security arrangements. The Police Commissioner had accompanied him, and now it was Mackenzie who introduced him to Rafael. The dictator's smile revealed silver teeth on each side of his mouth, and he did not trouble to extend his hand.

He said smoothly. "I am glad of your services, Mr Larren. I only hope that you can live up to your government's expectations. They seem to be convinced that you can keep me alive while on San Quito. You carry a gun of course?"

Larren smiled bleakly. "For this mission, yes."

"Good." Rafael turned to Mackenzie. "I think everything is satisfactory, Commissioner. There is no need for me to detain you any further."

"Thank you, sir." Mackenzie's face showed nothing of the dislike that Larren suspected was there, and the Scot turned to go. Davison, who had been lingering in the background, tactfully left with him.

Rafael turned towards the windows and gazed out into the smartly trimmed grounds of the villa. He stood for a moment until Davison had closed the door, and then he turned back and relaxed in the nearest armchair. He did not invite Larren to sit, but regarded the Britisher with dark, measuring eyes for several moments. Then he said.

"I suppose your superiors have already acquainted you with all the facts, especially the fact that someone very close to me is betraying my movements and has twice attempted to end my life?" When Larren made a brief affirming gesture he went on. "So, there is no need for me to elaborate, except to say that I expect you to discover the identity of that traitor. No doubt your Government does not consider that a necessary part of your job. Their only concern is that nothing should happen to me while I am here, and if my would-be murderer merely lies low until I return to Maraquilla, then they will be happy. But I must view the matter differently. I want that traitor unmasked, and if you succeed before I depart from San Quito I shall pay you a bonus of two thousand American dollars."

Larren said flatly. "That's very generous. But I understand that you suspect even your own bodyguard. Wouldn't it be best to dismiss all three of those men now, before the guilty one can make his third attempt on your life?"

Rafael gave him another hard appraising stare. Then he smiled thinly. "Yes, for you it would be best. You would borrow three more men from the Commissioner of Police and the next six days would go very smoothly. But afterwards I must still return to Maraquilla, and then I should have no protection at all. You think, perhaps, that I could hire new bodyguards, but on Maraquilla I could be no more sure of new bodyguards than I am of those that I have now. And besides, these three men have been loyal for a long time, and it is possible that the traitor is someone who is just as close on my personal staff. I cannot afford to dismiss three excellent men until I am sure."

He leaned forward and stabbed an angry finger towards Larren's chest. "Remember this, Mr Larren — you have been transferred to my employment, and from now on you will handle things as I tell you. My regular bodyguard will carry out their duties as normal, and you will simply join them. To restrict their movements in any way would only make the guilty man doubly alert, and it would be pointless for me to be perfectly safe for six days, and then go back to Maraquilla with the traitor still in my camp."

Rafael stared at Larren for a moment, and then he said coldly. "That is all. And now, perhaps you had best meet your colleagues." He raised his voice and snapped loudly. *"Hansen!"*

Almost immediately there were footsteps outside. The door opened and a tall, hard-faced man appeared. His drawling voice was unmistakably American.

"What is it, Mr President?"

Rafael said shortly. "Ask Sanchez and Friday to join us for a moment."

The American looked back over his shoulder, but the order had been heard and it was unnecessary for him to repeat it. Two more men had appeared beside him.

Larren turned slowly to face them. He already knew them all from Smith's careful descriptions.

The slim, dark Mexican was Sanchez Lorenzo. He was the least definable man of the three. His background was a vacuum that could not be traced beyond the two years that he had worked for Rafael. All that was known of him was that he could kill without conscience, and that he was an expert with a knife.

The brawny negro beside him was Samuel Friday, a solid muscleman of Caribbean origin. He had fought beside Rafael when the dictator had led the revolt that first gave him power in Maraquilla, and had remained loyal ever since.

Finally there was Reb Hansen, a loose-limbed Texan, as deadly as a sleepy rattlesnake. Hansen had fought in the Pacific with the American Marines before he was twenty years old, and since the war with Japan he had sold his killing abilities in a dozen other parts of the world. Now he was exclusive to Rafael.

Smith had warned bluntly: don't cross knives with the Mex; don't pit your strength against Friday; and remember that Hansen is probably the most lethal of the three. Now Larren assessed the faces of Rafael's private bodyguard and saw no reason to doubt Smith's judgement.

However, there was one point that Smith had missed, and that was that Jose Rafael was no more savoury than the killers he hired.

4

Red for Danger

LARREN could read hostility in each of the three faces as they were introduced by Rafael, and he knew that he could expect very little in the way of co-operation from his new colleagues. Sanchez and Friday watched their employer as he explained Larren's presence, but Hansen returned Larren's level gaze. It was clear that the news was an unexpected shock to all three, but no one moved or spoke until Rafael dropped a final bombshell.

He said calmly. "Mr Larren has been temporarily assigned by the San Quito Government, and they have requested that I grant him senior status. I have agreed to that request, and consequently Mr Larren will have complete control over my security for the next five days."

The statement drew an angry reaction from both Sanchez and Friday. Hansen's eyes simply narrowed and his gaze became more concentrated. Friday started to speak, but the snapping voice of the Mexican cut in before him.

"Do you mean, senor, that we have to accept this man's orders?"

"Precisely, Sanchez." The silver teeth glinted in Rafael's smile. "You have understood exactly what I mean."

Larren watched as Sanchez's thin lips drew tightly together, and although he knew that he should have expected something like this he inwardly cursed Rafael for his double-dealing smoothness. He had wondered how Maraquilla's President hoped to introduce a newcomer to his bodyguard without shaking the suspected traitor from his sense of security, but by making it appear that the offer of a fourth shadow had stemmed wholly from his hosts Rafael was neatly concealing his doubts of their loyalty.

The manoeuvring would have been admirable but for the stupid move in granting Larren senior status, for it was an empty title after he had been privately forbidden to curb the activities of his new colleagues. But even there, there was a twisted strain of reasoning, for by deflecting their inevitable resentment towards Larren, Rafael was hoping to make sure of his safety while at the same time declaiming responsibility. The fact that he was placing Larren squarely on the hot spot he clearly deemed irrelevant.

There was a moment of silence as Sanchez held his tongue, and then Friday said slowly.

"But why, boss? Don't we always take good care of you?"

"You take excellent care of me, Sam." Rafael smiled benignly at the big negro. "But it seems that on this occasion there is a very real threat to my life from some anti-government parties on San Quito. It seems that law and order is not maintained quite as — " He paused. "Perhaps strictly is the word. Yes — not quite as strictly as at home on Maraquilla. And so Sir Basil Trafford has become nervous and worries about my safety."

You double-talking bastard, thought Larren grimly. But he knew that there was nothing to be gained from arguing with the man who was now technically his employer, and so his unsmiling face remained totally impassive.

Rafael continued smoothly. "And now, if everything is clear, I think I shall retire to my bedroom and rest, I found the flight and that long lunch somewhat tiring." He rose to his feet and turned his silver-toothed smile directly at Larren. "I leave it to you to arrange the rotation of duties, but I suggest that now there are four of you you should work in pairs."

He nodded calmly at the other three men, and then strolled past Hansen and out of the room.

There was a long moment of silence after he had left, and Larren waited for one of the others to break it. Sam Friday looked uncertain but dangerous, a massive man in a dark blue suit with a pale blue shirt and a maroon bow tie. Both Sanchez and Hansen wore well-cut charcoal grey. Sanchez was standing to Friday's left, with his feet slightly spread and his arms at ease, his lips still hard compressed. Hansen had relaxed with his shoulders to the doorpost, and now he casually folded his arms and waited.

There was the sound of another door opening and then closing as Rafael entered his bedroom farther down the corridor outside. It was then that Friday moved.

The big negro stepped forward and slowly held out one huge hand. He smiled briefly and said.

"Well, man, if you're here to boss us then we'd best make you welcome."

Larren glanced down at the offered palm, noting the powerful fingers and thick wrist. Then he looked back at the negro's face, the smile was friendly but the eyes told him nothing. Larren smiled wryly and gently shook his head.

"That's nice of you, Sam. But I don't think I'll shake hands if you don't mind. You see, with a fist like that you could easily forget your own strength and crack my knuckles, and I wouldn't be much use to Rafael with only one hand."

Friday stared at him, and then the smile became a sardonic grin.

"Well now, if you ain't a smart one. How'd you guess I might do a thing like that?"

"Intuition perhaps."

"I thought only women relied on intuition." It was Sanchez who spoke. He came nearer as Friday turned scornfully away and his dark eye's fixed on Larren's face. He went on blandly. "Do you have any other feminine characteristics, senor Larren?"

Larren was aware of Friday's broadening grin, and of Hansen watching with silent amusement. Then he said softly.

"Only one, Sanchez. I'm sometimes more deadly than the normal male."

"So, you are also the big bad killer. I understand why senor Rafael has hired you. Tell me, for whom have you worked previously?"

"My loyalty is stable. It doesn't go to the highest bidder." Larren watched the Mexican's eyes as he spoke, but if the words scored offence then the fact did not register. Sanchez remained cool.

"Very noble, senor. But if you are a killer what are your qualifications? How many real live men have you killed?"

Larren smiled. "Sanchez, I don't like to be continually on the receiving end. If we must play questions and answers I'll ask you one. How many real live men have you killed? I understand that you have quite a reputation, but no one has actually witnessed you living up to it since you joined Rafael, and your past previous to that is very vague. Are you living on an unearned reputation?"

This time the Mexican's eyes did

register. His coolness vanished and his dark, thinly handsome face became vicious.

"Senor, my past is my own affair. And it does not pay to pry. And you will also do well not to doubt my reputation."

They faced each other for a moment, and then Friday chuckled from behind the Mexican's shoulder.

"You best remember that, man. This Sanchez, he means what he says."

Sanchez smiled briefly and stepped back. "Sam is speaking truly, senor. Remember that." He paused. "I wonder, senor, whether you have any reputation to live up to? Just how fast are you, senor Larren?"

"Fast enough, I think."

Larren sensed what was coming, and even as he murmured his answer his hand dropped swiftly to the front of his single-breasted jacket. The heel of his palm hit the butt of the Smith & Wesson 38 that he now carried at his waist, and the sharp impact caused the spring-loaded holster to kick the gun smartly into his hand. The automatic was sighted on Sanchez's belly in the same moment that the flash of steel appeared from the man's sleeve.

The Mexican stopped dead, his slim, fast-moving body suddenly rigid. The keen bladed knife in his hand was checked before its thrust had even begun.

Sam Friday had started forward in sharp surprise, but now he hesitated and stopped. Reb Hansen lounged against the door, still unmoving, but with the lines of amusement spreading more clearly across his face.

Sanchez breathed slowly, and then forced a reluctant smile.

"So you really are fast, senor Larren. That is useful to know on a job such as ours where we may become dependent upon each other's abilities." He shrugged his slim shoulders and carefully stepped back a pace, returning his knife to its sheath along his left forearm.

Larren slipped the Smith & Wesson back inside his coat and said calmly.

"Don't experiment with any more tests. The next time you may not get the benefit of the doubt."

Sanchez tightened his mouth, losing a little of his careless composure. Friday regarded Larren with grudging respect.

Then Hansen straightened his lazing body and drawled amiably.

"It was a nice exhibition, but I would have bumped him the first time."

★ ★ ★

After that first trial of strength the opposition became less marked. Sanchez concealed his fury, but as Hansen continued to remain indifferent to Larren's presence the Mexican and Friday slowly took their lead from the ex-Marine. Larren split them into two watches as demanded by Rafael, and decided on six hours of duty alternating with six off. But he did not attempt to act his so-called senior status beyond that. It was not necessary, and they were unfriendly enough already. He chose Friday as his own working partner, and paired Hansen with Sanchez. He reasoned as he did so that it was best to separate the two men who were most hostile towards him.

Apart from the reception on arrival Rafael's official visit was not due to start until the following morning, for it was assumed that Maraquilla's President would welcome an easy first day before the start of the tiring tour. And so for that first night Rafael was not expected to leave the villa Marola. The President was served a meal in his bedroom and afterwards announced his intention of retiring early. Larren and Friday remained in the main living room within hearing, while Sanchez and Hansen found their quarters.

Larren soon found the atmosphere stifling and the waiting boring. Sam Friday was a sullen, untalkative companion whose mood had dulled once his two friends had left. The negro had taken off his dark blue jacket and was sitting before a low coffee table with a pack of glossy playing cards spread out in a slow game of patience. His pale blue shirt had moulded to his muscled shoulders as he hunched forward to contemplate his game, and there was an automatic in the leather shoulder holster under his left armpit. Larren had noticed that Hansen and Sanchez had been similarly equipped.

When Friday had first produced the cards Larren had offered to join him, but the negro had grunted that he preferred to play solo. Now Larren idly turned the pages of a magazine. He read a sworn factual story of how two American G.I.s and four lush girls from an Amsterdam brothel had played a vital part in the winning of World War Two, and found himself half-wishing that he was one of those readers whose knowledge was so limited as to believe it. The rest of the magazine was on the same lines and he finally threw it away.

Twice during the first hours he got up to prowl silently through the darkened villa and around the thickly shaded grounds, leaving Friday alone while he checked that all was in order. Then shortly before midnight, when Hansen and Sanchez would relieve them, he decided to make the check again. When he announced his intention to Friday the negro simply grunted, and continued to deal out his cards. Larren put on his coat and moved quietly out into the corridor.

After he had closed the door behind him he waited for his eyes to adjust to the darkness. It was not quite absolute, for the night outside was again brightly lit by moon and stars, and as he had carefully memorised every detail of the interior of the villa he was able to move slowly without needing to switch on the pencil torch in his pocket.

He moved along the corridor away from Rafael's room. The villa was large and sprawling with accommodation for servants as well as for guests, and apart from the threat of an attack from inside Rafael's own party it was the servants that gave Larren most concern. There were five of them, coloured islanders who had been carefully vetted by Mackenzie. But even Mackenzie had been forced to admit that he could only be ninety-five per cent sure of their loyalty. The kind of money that Rafael's enemies could offer would be fantastic riches to these simple people, and they could be even more subject to fear than to greed.

However, the servants' rooms were quiet, except for the rasping snores of one of the occupants. Larren checked the rest of the villa and then let himself out into the grounds. He moved among the palms and flowering evergreen shrubs and made a complete circle of the inside of the surrounding wall. From time to time he stopped and listened, waiting until he heard a reassuring shuffle of movement or muffled cough from the native constables that Mackenzie had posted at intervals outside. His own movements were completely soundless.

At last he was satisfied and turned back towards the villa. A breeze rustled through palm fronds above his head and crickets whispered noisily in the long grass. He reached the villa and entered as quietly as he had left.

He had to stand motionless again to accustom his eyes to the deeper darkness, but not for so long this time. Then he moved back towards Rafael's bedroom and the adjoining room where Friday waited.

He was almost there when he heard the soft swish of movement and he sensed as much as saw the dark figure moving down the corridor ahead of him. Whoever it was was making unerringly for Rafael's door.

Larren moved swiftly and efficiently, closing with the unknown prowler in three fast, silent strides. There was a startled movement as the unknown tried to turn, and Larren dropped to one knee in a low crouch to avoid a possible shot at his chest or head. His left hand lunged forward to fasten on a slim ankle, and then the heel of his right palm slammed forward to thrust hard against a knee and send the unknown prowler crashing backwards. There was a high-pitched shriek that echoed above the sound of the fall, and in the same moment Larren sprang back and to his feet. His left hand moved deftly to brush down the light switch on the wall, while his right hit the automatic at his waist and brought it springing into his hand.

A second later two doors crashed open almost simultaneously. Sam Friday came through the first, just behind Larren's left shoulder, with his automatic jutting from a ham-like fist. And Jose Rafael burst through the other just ahead, his black hair tousled and wearing a pair of silk pyjamas.

All three stared at the gasping woman who sprawled on her back on the carpeted floor. Her short, wide-sleeved house-coat had fallen open at the hips and her long bare legs moved feebly as she struggled to regain her breath. She pushed herself up on her elbows and her long hair fell in a tumble of loose curls around her shoulders. It was fiery red hair, as dangerously red as the angry line of her vivid lips.

She said bitingly. "And what the hell do you think you're doing?"

Sam Friday chuckled softly and returned his gun to its snug nest beneath his arm. Larren still stared, his eyes cold. Then Rafael hurried forwards to help the girl to her feet, his face thunderous with anger.

"Yes, Larren," he said savagely. "Just what the hell do you think you're doing?"

"My job," Larren said bluntly. "Who is she?"

"Miss Keene is my — my secretary."

"Then why didn't you tell me you dictated letters in the middle of the night. I might have killed her." He paused suddenly. "Why haven't I seen her before?"

"Because she was ill on the plane flight," Rafael snarled. "Miss Keene suffers from air sickness. Hansen looked after her and saw her to her room while I was talking to you. She has been there ever since."

The girl was glaring hard at Larren as he slipped his gun back into its holster, and for a moment his gaze encountered her angry green eyes. Then she stiffened her body and drew her house-coat closer around her. Larren looked back at Rafael.

He said grimly. "I'll appreciate it, senor Rafael, if you'll keep me informed of any other visitors who might be expected to knock on your door in the night."

Twin spots of colour glowed in Rafael's dark cheeks and his eyes blazed. "There will be no other visitors. I can assure you of that. And bear in mind, Larren that your job is to protect me, and not to dictate in matters of my private life. I am not accustomed to such interference from a mere employee."

Without waiting for an answer he grabbed his mistress roughly by the shoulder and turned savagely away. The girl had lost one of her polished high heeled shoes during her fall, and now she almost over-balanced again as Rafael pushed her through the open doorway into his bedroom. The dictator followed her through and slammed the door violently behind him.

Larren stared for a moment at the closed door, and he decided then that this was one job that he was not going to enjoy. He would have preferred it if he had been sent to kill rather than protect Jose Rafael.

He turned then to see the grinning face of Sam Friday. The big negro was chuckling softly.

"I guess you just boobed, man," he said. His face was lit with satisfaction and he repeated. "I guess you really done boobed."

Larren remembered Smith's advice and resisted the temptation to hit him.

5

Death by Voodoo

THE white cock squirmed wretchedly on the large plate, its bright, frightened eyes glittering sharply in the moonlight. The head twisted from side to side and the baffled beak made repeated stabs in vain efforts to reach the tight cords that bound the feet and wings. A second bird, a white hen, lay similarly bound beside the cock on the plate. Apart from its trembling the hen was still, for its tiny brain had accepted before its mate the futility of pecking for the cords it could not reach.

The beat of the drums was rising in pitch, swelling in excitable rhythm that carried beyond the moon-splashed clearing, through the muffling foliage of forest and jungle, and almost to the outskirts of Aparicio several miles away. The drummers were beating with their bare hands, the hide topped drums gripped tightly between their knees. Their faces were concentrated and staring, the black skin glistening with the slow rivers of sweat caused as much by their own exertions as by the heat of the dancing fire close to the spot where the white birds lay.

A young native girl, her supple body naked but for a strip of scarlet cloth that fastened at her waist and fell forward between her legs, whirled swiftly to the rhythm of the drums. There was pure sensuality as the ruby glow of the flames passed and re-passed over the ebony movement of buttocks and hips, and complete abandon in the frenzied shaking of shoulders and breasts that increased with the tempo of the drums. The girl's eyes were bright and feverish and her face blank of all thought but the spur of ecstasy. The drums spun her faster and faster until her figure was a wildly spinning blur of movement.

And then, without warning, but with simultaneous precision, they stopped.

The dance continued for a few seconds longer, and then realization penetrated into the numbed mind and the girl stumbled to a stop. For a moment there was silence, and then her lips parted in a moaning wail that could have been of pain as she sank to her knees. She fell forward, one hand supporting herself against the earth, the other arm outflung with her finger directed towards the trussed birds.

On the edge of the circle in which she had danced stood a well-muscled negro who wore a pair of faded jeans and nothing else. His bare feet were spread apart and now he slowly unfolded his crossed arms from his bare chest as he smiled down at the girl crouching in the firelight. Then he moved to the large plate on the ground to which she pointed and lifted the white cock by its bound legs. The bird squawked and twisted furiously as he stepped back. Beside him now was the waist-high trunk of a cut-down tree, and on this crude altar lay an old brown-stained knife. The girl looked upwards, her lips trembling as she held her breath. The other watchers around the circle stared intently as the young man lifted the white cock high above his head, and reached for the knife with his free hand.

This was voodoo.

There was a murmur of suppressed excitement when the young negro finally cut the white cock's throat, draining the blood into a small cup. The girl in the firelight shuffled forward on her knees, reaching eagerly to dip her finger into the cup. The moon passed for a moment behind a cloud, and sudden darkness closed around the edges of the clearing.

From behind the inner ring of watchers Caroline Brand shuddered hard and closed her eyes.

The young coloured man who had brought her here gave her a quick nervous glance. Then his black hand touched her arm.

"Time to go now, lady," he whispered earnestly. "You got good story for magazine paper. No need to see more. Things get wild now. Much — much making love. Things not nice for white lady to see."

Caroline nodded with a feeling of deep relief, and allowed the young man, a porter from her hotel whom she had bribed, to lead her away. She most certainly had enough information for her report, although that report was not destined for the offices of the *London Mail*, or for any other newspaper for that matter. And she most certainly had no desire to witness an orgy.

★ ★ ★

The following day Simon Larren merged unobtrusively with the large party of officials who accompanied the two heads of state, Rafael and Dominguez, on the first leg of their tour of San

Quito. Rafael's original three shadows also stayed close at hand throughout the day, and there was also a disarmingly ordinary San Quitan police inspector named Barrios whom Mackenzie had detailed to cover Dominguez.

The morning was taken up with a visit to Aparicio's largest and newest school, which had been only recently opened. There was a negligible risk of danger from the carefully tutored children, careless of politics and seeing only an unexpected holiday from routine, and apart from keeping watch for any out-of-place adult Larren felt that he could relax. Lunch was provided in the school's brand new canteen, and Larren noticed Sam Friday melt silently away towards the kitchen where he would undoubtedly check on the food before Rafael sat down to eat.

The afternoon involved a tour of one of the largest sugar factories just outside the city, and here, with several hundred native workers still on the premises the shadowing detail remained constantly alert. Rafael was taking his time and asking lengthy questions which Dominguez and the factory manager took great pains to answer. The factory covered a wide area, from the large marshalling yards where the fresh-cut canes were unloaded in huge bundles from railway wagons, through the crushing machinery of the processing plant, and on to the massive circular silos where the raw sugar was stored. Beside the silos were large sheds where the extracted cane fibre accumulated before distribution as fuel or fertilizer. Rafael wanted to see it all, and seemed unaware of his luke-warm reception by the factory's working force.

There were a score of places where an intending assassin could have hidden, and although the area had been carefully investigated by Mackenzie's men Larren was not happy until the last smiles and handshakes had been played out. The whole party returned to the front of the factory where a fleet of cars waited, and

Rafael and Dominguez climbed into the gleaming Rolls Royce Silver Cloud which they shared. A police escort moved ahead of them and the rest of the entourage sorted themselves into the cars that followed. Larren and his three colleagues occupied a Daimler immediately behind the presidential Rolls. Mackenzie's man Barrios was with them. Sam Friday was at the wheel.

The drive back to Aparicio was uneventful and ended before one of the city's larger hotels where a civic reception had been arranged in the private banqueting hall. Here Rafael smiled his way smoothly through a score of introductions to Aparicio's leading citizens, and to the supporting members of Dominguez's cabinet. Carleton, the Deputy Governor, was there to represent Sir Basil Trafford, and Mackenzie loitered in the background. A lavish dinner was provided, followed by speeches all round, and afterwards Reb Hansen stayed close to

Rafael as Larren, Sanchez and Friday mixed casually with the other guests.

Larren was now feeling a little self-conscious of the spring-loaded holster that fitted snugly against his stomach. He had to keep his coat buttoned to hide the butt of the automatic that protruded above the waist-band of his trousers, and the atmosphere here was decidedly stuffy. He was not accustomed to wearing a gun, for usually they were uncomfortable and even a well-fitting shoulder holster was not wholly unnoticeable to a trained eye. He much preferred the silent knife that rested lightly against his breast. However, for this job a gun was a must, and he had to admit that the waist holster was the fastest and the best.

The atmosphere was now becoming informal, and white-coated coloured waiters were circulating with trays of savouries and drinks. Rafael was talking politely with a small, well-dressed woman whom Larren vaguely recognized as Vicente Dominguez's wife. Hansen was within six feet of the dictator's side, unostentatious but alert as he idly sampled a sardine neatly arranged on a sliver of toast. Friday was by the door, and Sanchez still circulated. Larren felt that all was safe and indulged in a martini from a passing waiter as his eyes surveyed the crowd.

Then a calm voice spoke beside him.

"Good evening, Mr Larren. I see that you're still doing your job."

He turned to look into the smiling eyes of Rafael's secretary, Miss Keene. She wore a low-cut evening gown of black silk, shot with threads of emerald, while emerald lace formed its full length sleeves. Her red hair fell in loose but smooth curving waves, and her mouth was a soft red line of enticement. The thought, red for danger, again entered briefly into Larren's mind.

He said evenly. "That's right, but at the moment it's having its compensations." He raised his glass meaningfully.

When he lowered the glass he said. "I suppose that you're looking for an apology for last night."

She laughed and shook her head. "No, I don't expect that. Somehow I don't rate you as the kind of man to waste time with apologies. Besides, it was really Jose's fault, he should have warned you to expect me. I was furious at the time, of course, but on reflection I decided that you could hardly be blamed."

Larren's gaze roamed beyond her for a moment, and then, reassured, returned to her face. He said easily.

"Perhaps I should apologize. I treated you rather roughly."

She smiled. "I think that maybe I like rough treatment. I'm not the fragile type."

Larren regarded her quizzically. "What type are you, Miss Keene?"

She said blandly. "The mistress type, but only for one man at a time. And at the moment I'm booked. There's a sign on me that says no trespassing." She paused. "But you can still cut out the Miss Keene business. My christian name is Rosemary."

Larren said calmly. "So, now I know your name — what else is there to know about you?"

Rosemary Keene smiled very gently. "Well, I'm an American citizen, and I'm free, white and twenty-one. But my dear old Kentucky mother was very, very religious, and when I didn't quite come up to her expectations I'm afraid I had to leave home. And beyond that I flatly refuse to incriminate myself." She gave him an appraising look. "But how about you, Mr Larren? Don't you have an easier name?"

"It's Simon," he admitted. "But there's no story."

"But there must be a story. Hired bodyguards are not quite like ordinary men. This for instance — " She reached suddenly for his right hand, drawing it towards her and then pushing back his sleeve and his shirt cuff to expose the deep slash of scar tissue across the back of his wrist. "How would an ordinary man acquire a wound like that? It must have come from some desperate fight or mission?"

"You're wrong," Larren lied blandly. "It happened in a simple accident. Somebody bumped me one night in Oxford Street and I pushed my hand through a shop window."

"I don't believe you," Rosemary replied. "But if you don't want to tell me anything about yourself, then I will tell you. You're not just another hired bodyguard, but an agent for the British Government. And you're only here to protect Jose while he's on San Quito. Isn't that right?"

Larren stared at her as he realized that Rafael must have taken her fully into his confidence, and slowly he forced down the surge of anger that was pointless anyway. It was becoming increasingly clearer that Rafael was completely indifferent to any embarrassment that he caused those around him. The dictator pandered only to his own egotism and vanity.

At last Larren slowly disentangled his hand from her fingers and said bluntly.

"If Rafael tells you everything, then it's hardly necessary for you to ask me."

"But Jose doesn't tell me everything. There are some things he doesn't know." Then she shrugged her shoulders and smiled sadly. "But I can see that I've irritated you by letting you know that you're not exactly incognito, so perhaps I had better go, and leave you to your bodyguarding. Do take care of Jose won't you, he's a pompous bear, but sometimes he can be a dear." She gave him a disarmingly warm smile and then turned away.

★ ★ ★

The day that followed was similar to the first, except that this time the itinerary covered the plantations of growing canes and other aspects of San Quito's basic sugar industry. Rafael inspected it all with a tireless show of interest, and continued to ask his endless questions. The day passed without a hitch and Larren noticed that Vicente Dominguez was gradually becoming more at ease. The job kept Larren almost as close to San Quito's President as it did to the man from Maraquilla, and he was able to sense some of the earnestness of the quiet, scholarly man's purpose. He felt that it was regrettable that Dominguez's ideals must inevitably fail.

There was another reception that night, but smaller and less time-consuming. By eleven o'clock it was over, and Rafael's party returned to the villa Marola. Rafael retired almost immediately to his bedroom.

Larren again took the first watch, partnering Sam Friday. The original three bodyguards were more amenable now, having seemingly decided to make the best of his unwanted presence. After he had out-manoeuvred Sanchez he believed he had earned a measure of respect, and only Rafael's stupid move in granting him senior status kept them still hostile. Except for Sanchez, of course. The Mexican would always be hostile.

However, Friday still preferred to play his cards alone, and so Larren lounged in an armchair with his feet planted against the wall. Once Larren got up to check through the villa and grounds, and twice he found his way to the kitchen and brought back coffee for Friday and himself. The second time the negro gave him a thawing grin.

"You should get some cards, man," he suggested. "It ain't no good two men playin' because you starts to concentrate too hard in case you loses money. And that way you gets tired and you ain't awake to the job all the time like you should be. But patience, now. That's different. It's interesting enough to make the time pass, but not enough to distract all your attention."

"Maybe you're right, Sam. I might get a pack tomorrow."

Friday shrugged and went back to sorting the cards, hoping for a black jack to match a red queen. Larren watched him for a moment and then carried his coffee back to his chair and sat down. He planted his feet against the wall once more and relaxed.

Three minutes later a blood-freezing scream ripped through the silence of the darkened villa.

The coffee cup crashed to the carpet as Larren tumbled to his feet, the Smith & Wesson springing into his hand. The big negro jack-knifed upright almost as swiftly, his cards cascading off the table as it was slammed aside by his knees. Both of them rushed for the door.

Larren was through it first, and without hesitation he lunged across the corridor and burst into Rafael's bedroom. The bedside light clicked on in the same moment as Rafael sat upright. The dictator was alone in the bed, his gold pyjamas open at the chest and strands of his black hair sticking stiffly across his forehead as he blinked in startled wakefulness.

"Lay flat, you fool! And switch off that damned light!" Larren fired the instructions crisply, and then hurried forward to douse the light himself. Rafael's mouth was weak with fear in the brief moment before the light went out, and then he did as he was told and let his shoulders press flatly to the bed.

Friday came into the room, stopping as he saw Larren cross to the window. Then the negro came swiftly to stand on the opposite side of the drapes. Larren opened them a few cautious inches, but no shot came through. He moved closer then and peered out across the darkened lawns. There was nothing to be seen. Then there was a disturbance from the corridor and Reb

Hansen appeared in his shirt-sleeves, an automatic in his fist. Sanchez was behind him.

Larren said sharply. "Where did that scream come from?"

"Servant's quarters." Hansen spared no words. "We came straight here."

Larren nodded in agreement. In their book it was the right move. Only Rafael was important. He said grimly.

"Reb, you and Sanchez stay here. Don't leave Rafael. Sam, stick with me."

Without waiting for any answers he thrust past Hansen and the Mexican and ran towards the servant's rooms. A heavy pounding at his heels told him that Friday had followed.

He found lights and confusion, and a medley of frightened voices. The most stable man there could only gesture to the window and say that whatever had frightened them was outside. Larren sprinted out into the grounds with Friday still in close support.

They separated, moving slowly, and

then the negro said suddenly.

"That way, man. Over there."

Larren looked towards the far corner of the villa grounds. There the palms and evergreens were thickest, and there, just above ground level and deep in the shadows was a tiny flickering of yellow light.

Together the two men moved towards it. There was silence now, except for the soft brushing of their footsteps through the grass, and Larren had the strange feeling that whatever had happened was over. Yet even so, there was a cold dryness in his throat, and he smoothed his free left hand lightly down his thigh to dry the moisture from his palm.

They reached the thick foliage above the yellow glow, and warily pushed inside the barrier of palm fronds and branches. A dozen tiny yellow flames shifted eerily in the slight breeze, and Larren sensed the sudden tightening of muscles in the big negro beside him. He crouched closer and his unsmiling face became cold and bleak and he had to swallow hard.

A man sprawled on his back in the long grass beneath the bushes. A man who was very clearly dead. There was a strangling cord still around his neck, cutting deeply into the bruised flesh. His face was waxen in the faint yellow light, but the swollen distortions of eyes and tongue made it unrecognizable. Only the fair hair, and the smart, double-breasted grey suit with the grey and red tie enabled Larren to identify the corpse.

It was Davison from the Governor's staff.

The pool of yellow illumination came from the tiny model of a coffin that was carefully balanced on the dead man's chest, for the miniature coffin lid was adorned with a dozen tiny, guttering candles.

Larren heard Sam Friday utter a choking sound beside him, and when he glanced up he saw that the massive negro was trembling and that his face had turned grey with fear.

Friday said hesitantly. "That — that cord around his neck. Man, I seen one of those before. It's made out of a dead man's innards. And I seen one of them coffins too. Man, that means voodoo!"

6

The Strangling Cord

LARREN crouched closer to examine the cord around Davison's neck, and despite the still warmth of the Caribbean night a cold wind seemed to pass through him. It was impossible to be sure in the faint glimmer of yellow light cast by the candles on that evil little coffin, especially as the cord was half buried in the swelling flesh. But the cord was fashioned from some white, gut-like substance, and Larren knew that in the history of voodoo it had been known for murders to be carried out with the gruesome strangling cords made from the dried human intestines of previous victims. He turned his head away slowly and saw again the greying pallor of Sam Friday's face. He knew then that there was no doubt whatever in the mind of the big negro. Friday was terrified.

Larren looked back at the body and there was a sudden tightness in his throat, a quick revulsion that was not so much at death, which he had witnessed many times before, but at the foul decorations that had been added afterwards. He sucked in a deep breath and puffed hard at the diminutive yellow flames. They keeled crazily and then went out, and Davison's twisted face became invisible in the abrupt darkness.

Without making any further attempt to touch the body Larren straightened up. Sam Friday had already backed away on to the open lawn, and Larren was glad to step back from the black shadows of the bushes and join him. The negro's eyes were darting nervously from side to side and the automatic was no longer steady in his hand.

Larren said grimly.

"Get back to the house, Sam. Put a call through to Police Commissioner

Mackenzie if it hasn't been done, and then stay by Rafael with the others. I'll look around a bit farther."

Friday hesitated, but it was obvious that he badly wanted to get back to the safety of the house and after a moment his pride caved in. He said hoarsely.

"Okay, man. I'll do that."

And then he turned and hurried back towards the villa. Larren watched him go and then continued the search alone. He was reasonably certain that there would be nothing else to find, and that whoever had dumped Davison's body would have made good their escape by now, but he had to be sure. A more thorough examination of the body was something that would fall in Mackenzie's province when the policeman arrived.

Swiftly and efficiently Larren searched the grounds. He would have welcomed a more powerful flashlight in place of the pencil torch that was all that he carried in his pocket, but the torch was adjustable and gave a strong light at full beam, and in any case he was relying mostly on his keen ears. He was feeling ill at ease, and he realized that the emanation of Friday's fear had reached out to influence his own straining nerves. Murder was an old companion, but voodoo was not. And that coffin had been too frightening.

However, Larren controlled his thoughts, and when he was satisfied that there was no further threat to Rafael in the villa grounds he made his way to the main gate. A native police sergeant opened it to let him out, and Larren questioned him briefly.

The sergeant answered simply. He had heard that first, single scream that came from the villa, but his orders had been to stay outside and ensure that nobody entered the villa grounds. Any internal disturbances he was to leave to Rafael's personal bodyguards. There was a telephone at the gate and he had used this to contact the villa and find out what was happening. Reb Hansen had answered and verified his instructions, warning him to keep himself and his constables outside the grounds in case Larren and Friday confused them with intruders.

Larren nodded approval as the sergeant finished, and then glanced at the two native constables who stood behind him. He said grimly.

"How many men do you have guarding the villa?"

"Six," the sergeant replied promptly. "That is including these two, but excluding myself."

"Then I think that you and I had best investigate the whereabouts of the other four. These two men can stay by the gate." Larren saw the look of hesitation come on to the sergeant's face and added pointedly. "Somebody has managed to break into the villa grounds, and out again. I want to know where and how, and what your constables have got to say about it."

He didn't say any more, for he sensed that any mention of voodoo would bring an even more scared reaction than he had seen on the face of Sam Friday. However, the sergeant's decision was a gesture of assent, and he ordered his two companions to remain on watch while he led Larren to check up on the other four constables who had been posted at intervals around the high wall encircling the villa Marola.

It took them exactly four minutes to discover that one of those constables had completely disappeared.

★ ★ ★

Fifteen minutes later Mackenzie arrived at the villa. With him came a small fleet of cars carrying a murder squad from police headquarters in Aparicio. The mixed party of English and San Quitan detectives hurried to the lonely corner of the grounds and methodically began to photograph and then examine the body before combing the area for any possible clues. Mackenzie made a brief, personal inspection and listened to a doctor's report before coming up to the house.

Simon Larren was waiting with Rafael and his bodyguards in the main living room of the villa. The dictator was now dressed and seated in an armchair, and his hand was steady around his third successive glass of neat cognac. Beside his chair stood Rosemary Keene, hastily dressed in slacks and blouse and looking slightly nervous.

Larren had not been fully idle while he waited for Mackenzie's arrival, and so he was able to give the Police Commissioner the few available facts. The servant who had screamed had been awakened by a tapping sound outside the window of his room. He had gone closer to investigate only to find a hideous voodoo mask framed against the glass. As he cried out the mask had vanished, and its wearer had presumably escaped from the grounds through the side gate where the missing constable should have been on duty.

Davison's body had presumably been carried through the same gate and been arranged before-hand.

Mackenzie's heavy-featured face was bleak as he listened, but before he could comment Rafael said sharply.

"Commissioner, who was this man? And why should the people who killed him go to such lengths to leave the body here, outside this villa, and then make sure that we would find it so quickly?"

Mackenzie said heavily. "The dead man was named Davison, he was a secretary on the Governor's staff. At the moment that's all that I can be sure about."

Rafael started to speak again, his dark face sour and arrogant, but then Larren cut him off. Rafael's eyes became angry at the interruption, but he snapped his mouth shut and allowed it to continue.

Larren said. "Sam told me that that nasty little coffin and the strangling cord were signs of voodoo, Commissioner.

Does that give any bearing on why Davison was killed?"

Mackenzie nodded. "On the face of it it's pretty conclusive. There's been a lot of voodoo revival on San Quito just lately, and Davison had some kind of theory that it was linked with the growth of Communism. The two seem to be going hand in hand and Davison was of the opinion that a lot of our recent troubles were as much the result of voodoo terrorism as of Communist provocation. Anyway, I know Davison was doing a lot of private prying into the voodoo subject." His voice became bitter as he finished. "Unfortunately I didn't take him too seriously. Now it seems that I should have done."

Rafael said tartly. "But how can there be a connection between Communism and voodooism? It is ridiculous. And in any case, why should the body be brought here?"

Larren said slowly. "I think I can see what Davison began to suspect. It's a Communist trick that I've encountered before. A few years back I worked on a temporary assignment with British Naval Intelligence in Hong Kong. The Communists there had revived one of the old secret tong societies to do their dirty work for them while they remained under cover. The new tong were just paid gangsters, but the old fear of the tong still existed and through them the Communists had a pretty effective control over the population. Here in the Caribbean I should imagine that the fear of voodoo would be even more effective, so it's not hard to believe that the Communists have enlisted the aid of a few high-up voodoo practitioners."

Even Rafael was listening now, and Larren was aware of the sharp interest of the others around him. Sanchez and Friday were eyeing him closely, and there was a speculative gleam in Reb Hansen's eyes. Rosemary Keene was looking at him as though he had abruptly become a stranger.

Then Mackenzie said. "It makes sense, Larren. It would explain why we've had so much trouble recently, and why there has been such an outburst of demonstrations against senor Rafael's visit. The Communists haven't got that amount of influence, and the bulk of the people are not poor or ignorant enough to want to believe their propaganda. But the voodoo fear goes very deep, and we've never quite extinguished the cults of the old gods." He paused and again bitterness tinged his voice. "Davison sounded too vague when he attempted to explain, but it seems clearer now. Especially in view of his death."

Larren said nothing. He was remembering how Davison had forced him to prove his own identity when he had first arrived, and the young man's fear that a substitute could have been planted at the airport. The fact had been glaringly plain then that Davison suspected a real and powerful threat to the security of the island, but because the young man had no official backing Larren had also failed to take him seriously. Now he was regretting the wasted opportunities he had had to question Davison more closely.

Rafael broke the silence.

"I take it that you have accepted this supposed link between Communism and voodoo. But, I repeat, why was the body brought here? Was it to scare me into cutting short my tour?"

Mackenzie hesitated and Larren answered.

"It's a possible answer, but it's more likely just an act of pure bravado to impress the local islanders, for the story's pretty sure to be spread. The very fact that the voodooists can penetrate into the guarded grounds of this villa and leave a corpse with all their ceremonial trappings will give them a high standard in a lot of susceptible minds. Perhaps in more normal times it would have been dumped in the gardens of Government House, but due to the interest in your visit leaving it here will clearly have more effect."

"I see." Rafael exploded the words

as though he had been personally affronted, and then he sipped angrily at his glass.

Mackenzie looked at him for a moment, and then he turned to Larren.

"What worries me is the purpose behind this," he said bluntly. "If they want to impress the islanders then it could be because they hope to prompt some kind of mob action. Things are getting damned awkward, and it might be best if this tour could be cut short." He faced Rafael. "With your permission, sir, I'd like to telephone the Governor and President Dominguez and make that suggestion."

Rafael waved a hand towards the telephone on a nearby table, and his silver teeth flashed as he spoke.

"Go ahead, Commissioner. But remember that I am not afraid for the tour to continue."

But it was only vanity that spoke, for Rafael's smile was not really a smile at all.

★ ★ ★

Mackenzie's call produced direct results, for Vicente Dominguez arrived at the villa within thirty minutes, and Sir Basil Trafford's car pulled into the grounds almost immediately afterwards. San Quito's President was badly worried, and he was showing it much more than the Governor who was serious but composed.

It was not Simon Larren's job to take part in such high level discussions as this, and so he remained mostly silent during the conference that followed. Mackenzie gave a solid, factual, policeman's opinion of the situation. He disregarded all political implications and stated that although he would do his damndest, and ensure that his men did likewise, he could not guarantee a trouble-free finish to Rafael's tour. Dominguez listened, but maintained that despite the complications of voodoo his people were still responsible and mainly loyal to the government. Rafael announced that he was prepared to go on.

Finally, when all opinions had been expressed, Sir Basil intervened.

"Gentlemen," he said precisely. "I think we must be severely practical about this. As I remember it the schedule for the next three days is as follows. Tomorrow, which will be Friday, President Rafael is to visit the blocks of new flats, some completed and some still under construction, on the west side of Aparicio, and in the afternoon he is to open the new stretch of road between the capital and the suburb at Jalipo Bay. On Saturday there is to be an inspection of the Army barracks at Caligas, and then a visit to the hospital here in Aparicio. On Sunday there is to be a final parade through the city and a service of thanks at the Catholic Church of St. Mary's. Is that not correct?"

Dominguez removed his glasses and nodded, an intent look upon his face. "That is so, Sir Basil."

"Then this is what I suggest." The big grey-haired man leaned slightly forward and his fist closed in the sharp, decisive gesture that Larren had seen before. "The schedule for tomorrow carries the biggest risks. There are nearly a thousand workers employed on those flats, and agitators could easily he slipped in amongst them, and there's sure to be another big crowd for the road opening ceremony. So, I propose that we cancel tomorrow's itinerary. We will announce that Senor Rafael had sprained an ankle or something similar. Something that will require a day's rest but no more. After that Saturday should be reasonably safe, the army is loyal and there is not much risk at the hospital. The Sunday parade will be the greatest danger, but we can decide upon that at the last moment."

Dominguez blinked his weak eyes, and then he smiled.

"I understand. We avoid the items with the biggest risk, but by not cancelling the tour altogether we do not concede victory to our enemies. Which is what they want. It is excellent. I am agreeable."

Sir Basil allowed himself a smile. Then he faced Mackenzie.

"What's your opinion, Commissioner? I know it's not exactly what you wanted, but Saturday should not provide you with too much of a headache, and if events warrant it we can always cancel the Sunday parade at the last moment." He saw that Mackenzie was still hesitant and added. "We can't just capitulate on this. If the population are given the impression that we, the government and the police force, are afraid of these voodoo terrorists and cannot protect our guests, then there could be hell to pay. The Communist position would he strengthened immensely."

Mackenzie sighed. "Aye, Sir Basil. I suppose you're right." Rafael said calmly. "Then the tour goes on. May I offer you gentlemen a drink?"

The announcement that Maraquilla's president had injured his ankle and was reluctantly forced to cancel his schedule for the day was broadcast by San Quito's radio station the following morning, and for the rest of the long hot day Rafael stayed at the villa Marola. The police guard around the outside of the grounds had been doubled after the previous night, and now they were fully alert. The fact that the fate of their missing comrade had not yet been discovered was a successful preventative against any slacking.

It was a tedious day. Rafael spent most of it in his room, dictating a maze of correspondence to Rosemary Keene. The four bodyguards again worked in a rota of pairs, two close and alert and two relaxing. Larren and Friday took the morning shift, and then handed over to Sanchez and Hansen at noon. They returned to their quarters and after a while Larren closed his eyes and slept, knowing that any alien sound would wake him.

Two hours later such a sound did draw him back into wakefulness. It was not a threatening sound and so he moved only his eyelids. He saw that Sam Friday had left his bed on the far side of the room and that the big negro was dressing carefully before the mirror. The only unnatural thing was that Friday had left off his shoulder holster, and was donning his jacket as though preparing to go off without it.

Larren said softly. "Going somewhere, Sam?"

The negro turned sharply, then gave a sheepish grin.

"That's right, man. Too damn stuffy in here. Nothin's goin' to happen while the boss stays put, and Reb and Sanchez can take care of him anyhow."

"Where were you thinking of going?"

Friday hesitated, then said brusquely. "That's my business, man. Don't go stickin' you're nose in. I won't be long."

He hesitated another moment, and then went out.

Larren waited a few moments in case the negro doubled back, and then he swung his feet to the floor and crossed to the window. He saw Friday striding down the wide gravel drive towards the villa gates, and then he swiftly reached for his jacket and shoes. As he fastened the laces he was remembering the original cause of his assignment, which was the fact that Rafael suspected a traitor in his bodyguard. And although the display of fear that Friday had shown at the evidence of the voodoo killing had not seemed significant last night, Larren was now realizing that a man who was afraid of voodoo was the one most likely to he suborned by the voodooists. It was a wild guess, for Friday had only just arrived on San Quito and there was no evidence to suggest that the power of voodoo could extend to Maraquilla, but the impulse to follow was strong.

Friday was out of sight as Larren

swung nimbly through the open window and dropped lightly on to the lawn outside. Larren moved fast however and the short cut enabled him to get within sight of the negro as the man reached the iron gates at the end of the drive. Friday exchanged a few words with the police sergeant on duty as the gates were unlocked, and then turned left outside the villa grounds.

Larren waited a few moments to give the negro a start, standing thoughtfully to one side of the drive in a patch of flowering shrub and palm shade. Then he continued at a casual strolling pace towards the gates.

The duty sergeant let him out without question, and he turned left in the same direction as the negro. The road sloped down-hill towards Aparicio and once Larren was out of sight of the villa he began to quicken his pace. It was a pity that there had not been time to avoid the sergeant, but Larren doubted whether the man had given any second thoughts to his close appearance at Friday's heels.

The air was dusty and hot, and Larren soon felt his shirt becoming damp across his shoulders. The strong, mid-afternoon sunlight was striking almost directly into his narrowed eyes and he was soon wishing that he had a hat. He hurried past more elegant villas, the gardens a riot of palm fronds, cacti and vivid splashes of purple bougainvillea. Then he caught sight of Sam Friday farther down the road.

The big negro was striding along strongly and not once did he look back. Larren kept him in sight as they descended the hill and entered the city, and he became gradually more and more dubious of his own suspicions. For despite his slight belligerence at the villa Sam Friday now moved with the deliberate carelessness of the completely innocent.

Larren had to move closer as they passed through the more squalid back streets of Aparicio, but Friday's attention was still directed unconcernedly ahead. The heat had emptied the streets and only a few people moved, few of them stirred from the patches of shade and there was an air of lazy poverty about the faded, crumbling buildings. An occasional car stirred the dust in the street and a thin dog nozed through a pile of rubbish beside a corrugated iron shack that had been built between two of the houses.

Larren wondered why Friday had turned off from the main road leading into the modern centre of Aparicio, and what business he had here in this run-down area of the old town?

The shadows grew longer and life began to grow sleepily from the siesta. More people moved in the streets, mostly indians or negroes, their eyes curious of the big black man in the dark blue suit, and of the white man who paced in his wake. And then at last the trail entered a quarter of seedy bars, and here Friday became hesitant, pausing as though he was not sure which building he wanted.

Larren stepped sideways into the mouth of a narrow alley, and waited while Friday made up his mind. The negro looked along the street, and then stepped from the cracked pavement and began to cross the road. He was looking up at a sign that read: BAR LAS VEGAS.

That was when Larren sensed the movement behind him, and in the same instant a slender blur dropped before his eyes and fastened cruelly around his throat. He was dragged backwards in a choking haze of cutting agony, and as the blackness surged through his brain he realized that he had been snared by one of the hideous strangling cords that had killed the luckless Davison.

7

Kill Or Be Killed

THERE was a band of fire around Larren's throat, and a savage drumming of blood in his aching brain. Consciousness began to return, seeping down to him slowly, and his body stirred with feeble movement. Then suddenly the memory of that sickly white cord of twisted intestine came rushing back before his eyes and blind panic infused his struggles. His body writhed as he forced himself back to full awareness.

He tasted earth, and smelled the wet mould of damp leaves against his face. His whole body was cold and there was a second tight pain around his wrists which were pulled behind him. With full awakening came control, and as he realized that the strangling cord was no longer around his neck he mastered the moment of panic and became quite still. Then a bare foot rolled him over on to his back and his bound wrists and he began to cough helplessly, each individual retching movement causing new agony in his throat.

When the spasm subsided and the tears cleared from his eyes he saw that it was night, and that he was lying in some kind of clearing that was enclosed by a black barrier of jungle. The foot that had rolled him to face the clouded sky belonged to a big dark-skinned man wearing old trousers and a ragged shirt. The man was young and his thick lips twisted into a scornful smile. The face was negroid, but not quite that of a full-blooded negro. The man was a mulatto.

Behind him were half a dozen others, all negro and mostly young, and all similarly dressed. But it was the mulatto who held Larren's attention, for he still held the strangling cord entwined around his thick, broad-fingered hands.

The mulatto chuckled as Larren's eyes searched his face. "You lookin' scared, white man," he said in English. "Is somethin' scarin' you?"

Larren didn't answer. There were a lot of things that he wanted to know, but he doubted whether they would tell him anything until they were ready and so he had nothing to say. Besides, his throat was too painful.

The mulatto took his silence as an admission of fear and again prodded him with his bare foot, rolling him playfully from side to side.

"You am scared, white man," he said triumphantly. "You really am scared." Then he laughed aloud and turned to his grinning companions. He made some derisive comment in Spanish that caused more laughter, and then began to give commands.

Larren was temporarily dismissed and left alone as the band of negroes busied themselves with gathering branches for a fire. Larren watched and guessed that they were making themselves comfortable as they waited for the arrival of somebody else — someone with more authority than the mulatto. His lips tightened and he tried to forget the drumming behind his temples and appraise his position.

He was obviously somewhere in the jungle covered interior of San Quito, but he had no idea of how far he had been carried since he had been throttled unconscious in the back alley in Aparicio. His captors were almost certainly voodoo disciples, but how and why they had captured him was a mystery, unless of course Sam Friday had deliberately led him into a trap.

His thoughts were blurred in his aching brain, and after a moment he tried to concentrate on his chances of escape. They seemed slim, for although his feet were free his wrists were very securely tied and he felt far from being fit. He knew that the Smith & Wesson had been taken from the holster at his waist, but a sudden feeling of hope flickered as he felt the slight pressure against his left breast. His captors had missed the slim knife concealed inside the lining of his jacket. However, even that was useless while he was unable to reach it.

The obedient negroes had got the fire going now, and their mulatto leader stood beside it with his arms crossed over his chest. The flames crackled and spat, and gave a growing light to the clearing. Larren examined his surroundings more closely in the spreading glow, and then he saw that he was not the only prisoner.

A second poor wretch was similarly bound and seated with his back against the bole of a tree on the far side of the clearing. The man's head was sunk dejectedly and his face was hidden, but the soiled uniform he wore made Larren realize that he was the missing constable who had vanished from his post outside the villa Marola the previous night.

The mulatto and his negroes were simply waiting now, and Larren closed his eyes and waited with them. For half an hour he lay there on the fringe of the firelight, ignored but for repeated stares to make sure that he had not moved, and slowly his head began to clear. At length he was able to consider the implications of his position again, but before he could reach any conclusions there was a sound of movement in the jungle.

He opened his eyes and saw that the mulatto, who had been sitting cross-legged on the ground, was now rising to his feet. He was facing the black tangle of foliage on the far side of the clearing near the bound constable, and his companions stared in the same direction. The native policeman's eyes were wide with fear and he cringed to one side as the rustling of approach drew nearer. And then suddenly two figures appeared from the darkness.

The first wore the elaborate trappings of a voodoo priest. His face hidden by a carved wooden mask that was surmounted by two curving horns. His body, like the mask, was garishly painted and his only apparel was a loin cloth. His throat and chest were draped with necklaces of shark's teeth and barracuda jaws, and from his belt hung two human skulls.

The new arrival stopped, facing the mulatto, and then the second man moved up beside him. The witchdoctor's companion wore a stained uniform of jungle green and his face was hollow-eyed and shadowed beneath an army cap. Behind them more negroes appeared, spreading out in a half circle around the clearing.

There was a brief conversation in Spanish with the mulatto, and then the two newcomers came slowly towards Larren. The mulatto gave a solemn order and two of his companions jumped to obey. Larren was hauled to his feet, and after a moment to regain his balance he stood there breathing evenly.

The voice from behind the mask spoke in perfect English, precise and amused.

"My colleague tells me that you are the new bodyguard employed by the President of Maraquilla." He didn't pause for the fact to be affirmed but went on. "Well, you are not the man I expected to find, but I think you may serve our purpose even better. Tell me, what is your name?"

Larren told him, and was pleased to find that his voice was not too hoarse, despite the burning soreness of his throat. A pair of dark eyes regarded him keenly through the slits in the mask, and then its wearer continued.

"It is somewhat fortunate for your friend Mr Friday that you followed him, otherwise he would have been here in your place. But — " The smile was evident, although unseen. "But not so fortunate for you."

Larren knew then that Friday had led him into a trap, but, it seemed, unwittingly. The men set to kidnap the big negro had recognized him as another of Rafael's bodyguards as he followed, and for some reason had taken him in Friday's place. It was plausible for he had accompanied Rafael in public often enough in the past few days to be easily recognized.

He said bluntly. "So you originally wanted Sam, but why? And who the hell are you anyway?"

The man behind the mask chuckled. "You can call me Doctor Medianoche. The name, if you are interested, means Midnight. It is a trifle melodramatic, but melodrama helps to impress my disciples. The name also indicates the hours of greatest darkness, the hour when many of our graveside rituals are performed, for of course you realize that grave soil is as necessary as blood to many of our rites. So you must see why the name seems fitting and significant to my followers."

"It's clear enough," Larren said grimly. "You use a bizzare name and filthy games to impress a few simple minds. But who is your friend?"

The man in the uniform was almost as tall as Larren and now his deeply sunk eyes blazed into Larren's face. He rasped harshly.

"That is not important. You need not know."

Doctor Medianoche laughed softly.

"The General is incognito, Mr Larren. He is merely a friend."

Larren said nothing, but the title of general had given him a clue. He remembered the rumour that Rafael's chief enemy General Savalas had landed with a boat-load of agitators somewhere on San Quito, and he was certain that this must be the same man.

There was a moment of silence, and then it seemed that the introductions were over for the masked doctor turned and rapped a string of commands to his men. The wide-eyed negroes flew to obey, two of them closing in to seize Larren's arms, while another group fell upon the bound and cowering constable on the far side of the clearing. The man gave a yelping scream as he was dragged to his feet, and then the scream was choked as a scrap of rag was rammed into his mouth. His eyes radiated wildly and despite his struggles he was hustled forward.

Medianoche turned back to Larren.

"Do you recognize the lost policeman from the villa Marola? He was very easy to remove, and if we had not known that there were four much more dangerous men guarding Rafael personally we could have killed the dictator then."

Larren said flatly. "That's as good as an admission that you did kill Davison. Why?"

"Because Davison was much too curious. The cult of voodoo has once again become a powerful force on San Quito, Mr Larren, much more powerful than the British authorities believe. Davison would soon have been able to convince them of this fact, and so he had to be removed. Leaving his body where we did, and as we did, was a nice refinement that has strengthened our control even more."

Larren's gaze fixed on the eyes behind the mask. He said calmly.

"Is that the whole truth. Or did Davison uncover some definite proof that this new growth of voodoo is backed by Communist party funds? And that voodoo is now not only a filthy religious cult but also a Communist tool?" He paused and then demanded. "What are you behind that mask, Doctor — voodoo priest or Communist agent?"

Medianoche stepped forward, his body tense with sudden fury. And then he retorted savagely.

"That you will see for yourself, Mr Larren. You will most certainly see for yourself." And then he turned and snapped again at his watching disciples.

Instantly one negro seized a flaming brand from the fire, and Larren's mouth dried in the sudden stab of fear that went through him. But the dryness was premature, for the man merely turned aside from the fire and began to lead the way out of the clearing. The garishly-garbed Medianoche followed with the silent General beside him, and then Larren and the captive constable were hurried along in the rear. More of the negroes grabbed burning torches from the fire as they passed and used them to light their way along a barely discernible path through the black nightmare of massed jungle.

Larren swallowed hard as leaves and fronds of palm slapped at his face, and despite the discomfort of thrusting hands he felt a sudden satisfaction as he realized that his last words to Medianoche had scored home. It was his only satisfaction as he was forced to stumble through the jungle night that was in pitch darkness beyond the sweeping movements of the torches. Roots and vines formed a tangling embrace round his feet, and once he plunged headlong only to be dragged immediately upright and hustled on again.

He began to wonder where they

were taking him, but the distance was too short to give much time for speculation, and after some five minutes of being forced along blindly the barrier of jungle suddenly ended. There was starlight, and sand under foot, and the unexpected sound of the sea told him that they had come out on the coast.

However, there was no respite, for the Doctor's willing helpers only grouped around him more closely as he was propelled down the beach. Their panting, negroid faces were flushed with excitement in the glare of the torches, and their eyes were eager with lust. They jostled him in a pack to the very edge of the sea.

They stopped where the waves swirled up the sand, and Larren saw then that there was a large motor launch waiting a few yards out on the black waves. Two negroes had already waded out with the struggling constable, and two more were already on the launch's deck, dragging the man aboard.

Medianoche had stopped on the wet sand and the General was beside him. The Doctor said sardonically.

"Would you care to join us, Mr Larren? There is to be a minor ritual that we wish you to witness." Then he laughed and nodded to the big mulatto who was foremost among his men.

The mulatto took over from one of the negroes gripping Larren's arms, and Larren was forced to wade out to the boat. The calm water was lapping around his waist when he reached it and he was dragged bodily on to the deck. He sprawled on the wet planking as the mulatto clambered up beside him, and then he saw that the General was also wading out to the boat. The masked Doctor was speaking firmly to the men still on the beach.

It was obvious that there was not room for everyone aboard the launch, for it was crowded even now, and the disappointment was bitter on the child-like expressions of the men who would have to be left behind.

However, they stayed back obediently when Medianoche left them to join the boat. The mulatto and one of the negroes pulled him reverently aboard.

The launch's engine started up, and after a moment it moved slowly out to sea. It pitched for a moment in the lightly-slapping waves, and then it gained enough speed to shoot through them as it roared out into the Caribbean. For a little over five minutes it ran at full throttle, and then, approximately a mile off-shore, it slowed to a stop.

Larren was hauled to his knees, facing the terrified native policeman who was crumpled in the launch's stern. Two of the negro voodooists dragged the second captive to a similar kneeling position, and the big mulatto stood over him with a large chunk of ordinary stone gripped tightly in his broad fist. The General watched. Doctor Medianoche stood upright, his arms folded beneath the lapping necklaces of teeth and skeleton jaws that hung low on his chest, his eyes regarding Larren through the slits of his mask. He said softly.

"What you are about to see is a simple voodoo execution." And then to the mulatto. "Continuada!"

The big mulatto smiled. He looked at Larren for a moment, and then he turned his attention to the man at his feet. His free hand twisted in the constable's frizzy hair and viciously turned the staring face upwards. The man's eyes were fearfully distended and he struggled helplessly against the restraining hands and the crude gag. A muffled scream sounded in his throat and was trapped there as the mulatto deliberately smashed the heavy stone against his right ear.

There was a horrible fascination in that suddenly bleeding flesh, and Larren's gaze was riveted as he watched the broad trickles of red flowing down the whimpering man's dark neck. And then the mulatto took a small bag from his belt and poured a trickle of greyish powder into his palm. He slapped his palm hard against the constable's head and rubbed the powder cruelly into the torn flesh of the crushed ear.

Larren tore his gaze away and stared angrily at Medianoche.

"It is poison." The Doctor explained calmly. "Even if the blood does not attract the sharks and barracuda, the poison will take effect before he can reach the shore."

Larren's muscles stiffened, but the men holding him tightened their grip and he was held still. He looked back as the mulatto cut the cords binding the constable's wrists and the doomed man was pushed to his feet. He clawed at the rag in his mouth and screamed hysterically with the sudden freedom, and then willing hands seized his writhing body and pitched him over the launch's side into the sea.

Larren tasted salt from the splash of spray as the man went under, and then the pitiful screaming began again as the man returned to the surface.

For a moment he floundered near the boat, and then he began to splash away towards the mile-distant shore. His cries had stopped, but his murderers listened with an intentness that expected more.

And then the last scream came, a note of desperate agony that could only mean death. Its echo hung in the night long after the sound itself had stopped.

Medianoche said calmly. "He is fortunate, the barracuda are quick tonight."

Then the evil mask looked for a moment at Larren, and then he nodded to the mulatto.

Sick fear swamped through Larren's body and he fought with unavailing fury against his captors. The big hand fastened in his hair and his head was wrenched to one side. The mulatto was grinning and the blood-stained stone was poised.

And then the General broke his long silence.

He said softly. "That will do. I think Mr Larren has now been sufficiently frightened."

The mulatto glanced at his masked master, received a nod of acknowledgement, and then he stepped reluctantly back. The General moved closer to take his place, staring down at the kneeling Larren.

He said bluntly. "I think you realize how ruthless my friends can be. So now I give you a choice. You can die as your fellow-prisoner has just died — or you can be released on the condition that you undertake to kill President Jose Rafael."

8

Friday's Secret

LARREN looked up into the General's darkly-shadowed face, staring into the unblinking glitter of those deep-set eyes. The sweat was growing cold upon his body, and for a moment the sense of reprieve had been so great that he had failed to understand. The General's words had not quite registered in his throbbing brain, but now the marked purpose in those confident eyes made everything clear. They had planned all this for Sam Friday, believing as Larren had done that the negro would be the most susceptible to voodoo threats and to the demonstration of voodoo power, but at the last moment the mulatto had recognized a better opportunity in Larren. The man must have known that

Friday had worked for Rafael for a long time, and that it was possible that his loyalty would be too deep-rooted to crack, whereas it was reasonable to assume that the man most recently hired would be the one with the least amount of loyalty towards his employer.

The thoughts crowded through Larren's head, but overriding them all was the fact that his captors were silently awaiting his answer. The big mulatto stood with his bare feet splayed against the slight movement of the launch, his arms at his sides and the fingers of his right hand still curled around his executioner's stone. Medianoche's arms were still folded across his bare chest, his eyes gleaming through the ghoulish mask that hid his face. The remaining voodooists watched like a set tableau in black wax, their bodies still and the breath hushed in their throats. The General's tight lips were unrelenting.

Larren reach his decision and

swallowed hard. He said weakly.

"All right, if that's what you want — I'll kill Rafael."

Satisfaction eased the General's mouth, and then came an ugly smile.

"Of course you will. That is exactly what I expected you to say. But how can I be sure that you will keep that promise once you have been released?"

Larren lowered his gaze and said dully.

"I don't doubt that you've thought of something."

A chuckle sounded behind the voodoo mask and Medianoche said. "Correct, Mr Larren. We have decided to set you a deadline. You have until midnight tomorrow to assassinate the dictator. The hour and my name are synonymous, so you cannot possibly forget. If Rafael is still alive at that hour, then your death is assured."

Larren shifted uncomfortably and the General continued. "I think tonight's performance should have convinced you of our sincerity. And don't doubt that the Doctor's disciples can pick you up again if you fail us. You are not as heavily guarded as your employer, and we can force any native on this island into becoming our ally."

He paused, and then added. "But to prove that we are not completely barbaric I will include another small incentive. If Rafael dies before the deadline, you will not only live, but will receive a small bonus of five thousand American dollars."

Larren looked up then, he coughed to clear his throat, and then said.

"All right, I said I'd do it. But how am I supposed to kill him? There are still three other bodyguards."

"That is your problem. I hope you can solve it." The smile returned momentarily to the thin mouth, and then vanished again. "It is agreed?"

Larren nodded slowly. "It's agreed."

The General hesitated a moment, staring hard into Larren's face. Then he glanced away at Medianoche. The Doctor made a sign and Larren was released and allowed to get up from his knees.

For a moment Larren stood unsteadily, and then a knife passed smoothly between his wrists, the steel pressing cold against his skin, and then he was able to bring his hands away from his back. He shook off the cords and massaged the deep grooves they left with wincing fingers.

Medianoche said calmly. "The mulatto and his companions will escort you back to the outskirts of Aparicio, and then return the gun that was taken from you. After that you will be on your own."

Larren nodded without speaking, and he kept his eyes fixed on the wet planking of the launch's deck. Now that his hands were free he was remembering the knife they had missed that was still concealed in his jacket, and the desire to kill was fierce and savage in his heart. But he was badly out-numbered, and although he knew that he could account for the masked Doctor, and possibly the General too, it would prove an unnecessarily fatal mistake now that they intended to release him. And so he kept his face downcast in case the grey-green fury in his eyes betrayed the thoughts in his mind.

Medianoche gave an order, and the General returned to his seat in the stern as the launch's engine roared and her bows began to pierce the black waves on the start of her run back to the dark shoreline of San Quito.

★ ★ ★

It was two hours later before Larren was once again outside the heavy iron gates to the villa Marola. The police sergeant on duty knew his face and let him through, and as he approached the villa itself he saw Mackenzie's car standing in the drive near the verandah and guessed that his absence had been reported.

The doors were unlocked, and he let himself in without knocking. Almost immediately the light flashed on, and beside the wall switch stood Sanchez Lorenzo with a quickly levelled automatic in his hand. The Mexican stared, and then pushed the gun back inside his jacket.

"So the senor has come back. Where the devil have you been?"

"At the bottom of the garden, playing with the fairies," Larren said tartly. "Where's Rafael?"

Sanchez looked angry but he answered.

"Senor Rafael is in the main room with the Commissioner of police. Sam and Reb are with them."

Larren voiced his thanks and headed in the direction indicated, and after a moment of hesitation the Mexican followed.

Without ceremony Larren pushed open the door. Sam Friday was across the far side of the room and the negro took a quick step forward. The lounging Hansen moved alertly in front of Rafael who was seated and facing the heavy figure of Mackenzie. The

Scot had twisted in his chair. For the space of seconds they stared at him, and then relaxed. Reb Hansen gave a slow smile and then moved aside to reveal the narrowed eyes of Rafael.

The dictator said sharply. "Larren, you have been missing for eight hours. What has happened?"

Larren realized that it was time that he too relaxed, and forced a tight smile.

"Quite a lot," he said. "It's been an interesting evening." And then he walked over to the tray of bottles by Rafael's side and deliberately poured himself a stiff measure of Haig."

Mackenzie laid down the cigar he had been smoking and said bluntly.

"You've caused us a spot of concern, Larren. So perhaps you'd best tell us what has happened."

Larren allowed the warm fire of the Haig to flow smoothly down to his stomach, melting the last of the tension inside him, and then he told them.

Rafael listened, his thin face marked

with sudden shock, and when Larren had finished he said harshly.

"Am I to understand that you have agreed to assassinate me in return for your own life?"

Larren smiled grimly. "It was the logical, and only thing to do."

"But — "

"Mr Rafael," Mackenzie interrupted. "It's surely clear that Larren doesn't intend to keep his side of that agreement, otherwise he'd hardly be telling us all about it." He looked at Larren then and his eyes were grave. "I suppose there's no doubt that the man they killed was my constable?"

Larren said quietly. "I'm sorry, Commissioner. There's no doubt at all."

Mackenzie nodded soberly. "Aye, I thought not." Then his tone hardened. "Can you describe any of these murdering animals?"

Larren described the mulatto, and then went on. "The others were just trash and rif-raf. The man who called himself Doctor Midnight was negro and spoke perfect English, and sounded cultured and educated. The fact that he used that mask to keep his face hidden all the time suggests that he might be someone fairly prominent."

He stopped there, and then finished. "That only leaves the so-called General. He was about my own height, wearing army uniform. His eye sockets were very deeply sunk in his face." He swung round on Rafael. "Does that sound like your friend General Savalas?"

Rafael's face was again marked with shock, and his head nodded slowly.

"It sounds exactly like Savalas. But what do you know of him?"

"Not enough," Larren said flatly. "What can you tell me?"

"Only that Savalas is my biggest rival. On Maraquilla he plotted to turn the army against me, and when I sent men to arrest him he managed to escape. Since then he has been in hiding, but continues his attempts to gain power. But what is he doing here on San Quito? How did he get here?"

Mackenzie answered that.

"He came by boat, with a party of his friends. We heard the rumour that he was here but this confirms it." His square face was bleak as he went on. "And now it seems that he's joined forces with these Communist voodoo-men, or whatever the hell you would call them. And they all want you killed, Mr Rafael. Savalas, because he takes over in Maraquilla. And the others because your death would cause trouble to topple Vicente Dominguez and his government, and leave room for the Communists to take over here in San Quito."

Rafael's face was just a little scared, and then the silver showed in his teeth as he smiled briefly.

"You present the facts well, Commissioner. But if I cut short my visit and return to Maraquilla, Savalas will only follow me there. So for me such an act is irrelevant. And for you — " He smiled again, but this time more boldly.

"Your problems are simply solved by ensuring that I remain alive."

Mackenzie maintained a grim silence, and Larren realized then why Rafael was determined to see the tour through to the bitter end. On Maraquilla there was no one whom the dictator could fully trust, while here he had a British agent and the whole of Mackenzie's police force to attempt his protection. Clearly Rafael was hoping that his problems could he finally solved before he left San Quito.

Mackenzie saw it too, and he rose slowly to his feet.

"We'll do our best, Mr President. The security arrangements are as tight as I can make them, but I'll get back to headquarters and see if we can't do something about finding your friend Savalas, and the voodoo-laddie who calls himself Doctor Midnight." He bid them goodnight, and then he said.

"Now that you're back, Larren, you'd best see me off the premises."

Larren nodded, and he walked with

the heavy Scotsman to his car. A police chauffeur was waiting at the wheel, but before they were close enough for the man to hear Mackenzie stopped. He reached into the inside pocket of his jacket and said.

"There's a message for you from London, Larren. It doesn't mean damn all to me, but that's what made me think it might be important. I wasn't sure whether you'd want Rafael and company to know." He handed Larren an ordinary telegram form and waited.

Larren unfolded the single sheet, and it took him a moment to realize that it referred to something he had all but forgotten: his request for information on Caroline Brand. The answer was in one line.

Simon. Negative report. Harry.

It meant that London had been able to find nothing to suggest that Caroline was not a legitimate news photographer working for the *London Mail*.

Larren looked at Mackenzie and said.

"It could have been important, but it's not. Thanks anyway."

Mackenzie nodded and then got into his car. He said a brief goodnight, and as he drove away Larren knew that San Quito's solid Commissioner of Police was a badly worried man.

* * *

There were still several hours before dawn, and for the rest of the night Larren rearranged the watches, partnering Friday and Hansen in order to give himself a few hours sleep. The arrangement was accepted without comment, and Larren returned to his room, which was now empty with Friday absent.

However, Larren was not unused to long stretches without rest, and he had one more job to do before he finally slept. He waited until he was sure that Sanchez was sleeping in the next room, and then he again left quietly through the window. So far he had kept silent the fact that he had been following Sam Friday when he had been ambushed, and now he wanted to find out where the negro had been going. And if possible, how the voodooists had known of his movements.

The police sergeant at the gate was surprised to see him, but Larren had no hesitation in using the threat of Mackenzie's wrath to ensure the man's co-operation and silence. Once outside the villa grounds he moved faster until he was able to hail a cruising taxi on the outskirts of Aparicio. The taxi was a stroke of genuine good fortune at that late hour, and fifteen minutes later he told the driver to stop in the street adjacent to the BAR LAS VEGAS. He instructed the driver to wait, and then continued on foot.

As he had expected in this quarter the bar was an all night place, there were still lights inside and the sound of music. The usual curtain of hanging beads draped the doorway, and all of

Larren's senses were fully alert as he cautiously pushed them aside.

Beyond, the interior of the bar was almost empty, and badly lit. The tables were cheap and uncovered, the chairs untidy. A drunk slumped in one chair by the wall, and two near-drunks occupied one of the tables. A bored girl with an over-painted mouth leaned against the bar. The sole barman looked drowsy as he moved a cloth over the counter. The music came from a transistor radio on a shelf behind him, and cigarette smoke still stained the air, although no one was now smoking.

There was nothing to cause alarm, and Larren moved to the bar. The barman met his eyes, unconcerned, and then stirred himself to answer Larren's demand for a scotch. Larren wondered why the hell Friday had needed to come here?

Then the girl with the over-painted mouth noticed his presence and came nearer. She wore a tight bodice that almost pushed her full breasts out of a loose blouse, and she smiled an ageless smile.

"Beunas noches, senor. Do you look for one of the other girls, or are you going to buy Rosita a drink." Her hand touched his arm and she drew a deep breath that proudly displayed her breasts. And then she relaxed and smiled again. "Rosita is the cleverest girl here, senor. She knows tricks that are not even written in the Kama Sutra."

Larren stared at her, and then abruptly he laughed, wondering how on earth he had missed the glaringly obvious. For the BAR LAS VEGAS was simply a brothel.

9

An Old Friend

THE following day, Saturday, the fast deteriorating goodwill tour of San Quito continued. Rafael inspected a military guard of honour at the army post of Caligas, a small township some thirty miles inland from Aparicio, and afterwards, guided by the Camp Commander, a Colonel Oparto, inspected the post itself. Then after lunch the cavalcade of official cars retraced the dusty drive back to the capital to visit Aparicio's largest hospital. The President of Maraquilla concealed the strain that he must have been feeling beneath his usual flow of smooth questions, but his host was more obviously ill at ease.

Perhaps the last thing of which anyone could have accused Simon

Larren was the ownership of a soft heart, but even Larren's sympathies began to strengthen towards the disillusioned President of San Quito. It was clear now that Vicente Dominguez had faced reality, and that he knew that this first of his planned exchange of goodwill visits was also to be the last. For even if the joint opposition of Trafford and Mackenzie were to allow him to extend another invitation, it was doubtful that any other Caribbean leader would accept.

All that Dominguez could hope for now was that the threatened violence would not erupt during the next two days, and that the island could be brought back to normal and his own image restored after the tour was over. And even that hope was in the balance, for there had been more demonstrations and disturbances in different parts of San Quito, and there were conflicting rumours that Communist forces were prepared to take advantage of any incident. The situation was still that of the powder barrel with its many fuses, only now every fuse was burning on the last few inches.

However, although Dominguez had every right to be inwardly bitter at his own clumsy choice of the man who had presented such perfect opportunities for his enemies, he still remained unfailingly courteous to his guest. Only the slight traces of anxiety betrayed his inner feelings as he accompanied Rafael.

Simon Larren remained constantly alert throughout the long day, although his mind still grappled with his thoughts. He was distrustful of his three fellow-bodyguards, and he watched them almost as closely as he watched Rafael. When he had left the BAR LAS VEGAS last night he had been satisfied that Sam Friday's earlier visit had been harmless if not innocent. It had seemed plausible that Savalas could have known of the negro's habits, and somehow, possibly by arranging for some voodoo-controlled servant at the villa Marola to recommend the place, he had been able to anticipate Friday's trip to that particular bar. But that had been last night, and now, on reflection, Larren was beginning to wonder whether he had accepted too easy an explanation.

He knew that he could probably get at the truth by questioning either Friday himself or the villa servants, but that would only tell the negro that he had been spied upon, and Larren did not want that to happen just yet. The other two shadows had aroused no cause for suspicion. Sanchez was cold and efficient, although he still remained hostile, while Hansen seemed even more alert in his own casual way. However, it was the very fact that their every move was so perfectly in order that made Larren uneasy, for he knew from experience that men of their type were never completely blameless.

If there was to be an attack on Rafael from inside his own bodyguard then Larren still had no idea of from which direction it was likely to come.

★ ★ ★

That night, at the end of the last full day of the tour, there was a final dinner reception at Government House. It was attended by basically the same guests who had appeared at the previous dinners during that week, and was mostly in the nature of a farewell party. Speeches were made by both Presidents, by Sir Basil Trafford, and by half a dozen lesser personalities. Toasts were drunk, rather bitterly by some, to the continuing goodwill between San Quito and Maraquilla, and then to Her Majesty The Queen. The guests then moved from the dinner tables to the large hall, where a small dance combo made a bowing appearance in frilled shirts of yellow silk, and drinks continued to be served.

Rafael immediately made a polite bow to Dominguez's wife. The lady smiled and rose and together they moved among the dancers. Larren saw Rosemary Keene watching, and then

Reb Hansen touched her arm and spoke quietly. Rosemary nodded, her red tresses swirling slightly as she did so, and then they too moved into the crowd, casual, but always close to Rafael.

Larren briefly scanned the rest of the crowd. Sir Basil was dancing with Lady Trafford. Carleton, the Deputy Governor, was talking to Mackenzie. Sam Friday was slowly and watchfully circling the perimeter of the dance floor, looking vaguely uncomfortable in the black evening dress he now wore. Sanchez, again in evening dress, stood by Dominguez while he patiently awaited the return of his wife. Dominguez's man Barrios was with them. Everything seemed perfectly safe and controlled.

Larren straightened the smooth lapel of his own dark tuxedo and strolled towards Mackenzie. Carleton moved away as he approached, leaving the Police Commissioner alone. Mackenzie wore a white evening jacket with a red bow tie, and looked as though he was finding the outfit warm. As usual there was a cigar in his hand.

Larren said quietly.

"What do you think, Commissioner? Is it likely that there's a Communist, or a voodooist, or even a homicidal waiter here tonight?"

Mackenzie looked round and shrugged without smiling. "It would surprise me," he said. "I checked the guest list myself, and about the only thing I haven't had done to the waiters is to turn them upside down and shake them. Even if they are homicidal there's not one of them could have sneaked a weapon in here tonight." He paused a moment, and then finished seriously. "But I've got the place well covered, and I'm ready for surprises just the same."

Larren nodded and said slowly.

"It's as well to be prepared, but somehow I don't think that anything is going to happen tonight — even though it is the last night of the tour.

Savalas and Midnight gave me a twelve o'clock deadline before I'm supposed to kill Rafael, and I think they'll wait until then before they make any more moves."

"I'm not so sure," Mackenzie said bluntly. "It may be that that's exactly what they want us to think. And anyway I'm a long way from believing that those two laddies are the only cause of our worries."

Larren thought about it, then answered.

"You may be right, but I'm still more worried about tomorrow. We don't get rid of Rafael until the afternoon, and I haven't been told yet that we're cancelling the parade before the morning church service."

"And you won't — " Mackenzie drew a heavy breath. " — because we're not. I wanted it cancelled, but in spite of everything Sir Basil and President Dominguez want it to go on. They still think they can get away with it and save some political face."

He spoke the last two words as though they tasted sour.

Larren frowned, and then asked.

"Have you had any success in tracing Savalas? Or in getting a lead to uncovering Midnight's identity?"

"None at all," Mackenzie replied. "I've had some of my best men asking questions in every back street in Aparicio, but no one will give any answers. They're all afraid of voodoo. But at least that has made one thing clear, and that is that these voodoo people have a really strong hold over the mass of the population. I didn't even realize that until a couple of days ago, and now I'm not even sure that I can trust some of my own native constables. And I don't like it. Not one damned little bit."

Larren understood the Scotsman's feelings only too well, but at that moment he saw Carleton returning and after nodding briefly he moved tactfully away. He noted that Sanchez and

Hansen were still close to Rafael and realized that this was an unchanging pattern, Friday, the most noticeable man of the three, was still circulating among the guests. Larren continued his own prowling.

He searched hopefully for the beautiful redhead, Rosemary Keene, for he was still very curious about Rafael's mistress, but when he saw her she was dancing with one of Dominguez's fellow ministers. Larren smiled wryly and turned away, and collided gently with an old friend.

She was again wearing the light pink costume she had worn on the plane, but now the attractive red hat was missing from her dark gold hair. She wore no gloves and an expensive Rollieflex fitted with a silver bowled flash attachment hung from a leather strap around her neck. Her deep blue eyes regarded him sternly.

"Simon Larren," she said. "I thought that you were going to telephone me at my hotel? It's been four days since

159

our plane landed, and I haven't heard a word."

For a moment Larren registered surprise.

"Caroline," he exclaimed. "What are you doing here?"

"That was going to be my next question for you," she replied warmly. "It seems to be our stock conversation, doesn't it?"

"Yes it does," Larren was smiling now. "If the world gets any smaller we two will be crowding each other off the edges. But what are you doing here?"

She raised the camera. "I'm a working girl, remember? I've got a special pass from a really darling secretary on the Governor's staff that lets me in to take press pictures. I'm hoping to get some intimate shots of the two Presidents later in the evening." Then she added severely. "But not the kind of intimate that you usually think about."

"You misjudge me," said Larren

sadly. And then. "I've only just met you, so I take it that you've just arrived?"

"You're so brilliant and so right. And you're also trying to steer me away from the questions I asked you. Why haven't you phoned? And what are you doing here, hob-nobbing with the cream of San Quitan society when you're supposed to be handling a big business deal?"

Larren smiled. "I'm just fortunate. My business associate happens to be part of the cream, and he wangled me an invitation. I'd introduce you but — " He looked around vaguely. " — But he seems to have vanished at the moment. I think he was dancing with one of the ladies."

"Very good." Caroline clapped her hands in light applause. "And now tell me why it is that every time I've looked through my camera to take pictures of the Presidential party during the last few days, you have always been somewhere in the viewfinder?"

"Now that's an exaggeration," Larren said blandly. "You may have seen me once or twice because one of the members of President Rafael's party has also shown an interest in one of our export lines. He has connections with an import firm in Maraquilla and I'm trying to sell him a ship load of bicycles. You'd be surprised at how big a market there is for bicycles in a country where they can't afford cars."

Caroline smiled. "Which one is this bicycle millionaire?"

"The American, Mr Hansen." Larren took her arm and pointed out Hansen who was still lounging close to Rafael's side. But at the same time he knew that his explanation, even though it had been prepared beforehand for just such an emergency, was totally inadequate. It wouldn't stand up to any more questions, and so he didn't give her the breathing space to ask any.

He moved in front of her and went on smoothly.

"But in any case, Mr Hansen will

162

be flying back to Maraquilla tomorrow with President Rafael, and my business with the San Quito firm is already finished. So unless you've found some handsome Spanish escort to console your loss during the past few days, I'm perfectly willing to buy you a dinner in the evening. They tell me that there's a perfect swimming beach just a few miles outside Aparicio that's faced with the most ritzy restaurants, and the Caribbean moonlight is the most romantic in the world."

Her smile was radiant.

"Simon, I'd love to, but — "

"But I never listen to buts," he interrupted. "I'll telephone tomorrow afternoon to let you know what time I'll be arriving at your hotel. And incidentally — " He entered the bold lie without the slightest trace of remorse. "It won't be the first time that I've called. But on the other occasions you were always out. The hotel switchboard must have forgotten to tell you."

"Oh," her lips rounded and her eyes softened. "Simon, I didn't know. I'm sorry if I sounded reproachful."

Larren was spared the necessity of answering by the arrival of one of the Governor's assistant secretaries who coughed discreetly and then announced that His Excellency and the two Presidents were ready for Miss Brand to take her pictures. Larren repeated his promise that he would call the following afternoon, and breathed a sigh of relief as she was led away.

* * *

Later, as he kept watch with Sanchez at the villa Marola, Larren's thoughts were still with Caroline Brand. He had diverted her interest once, but now he was beginning to wonder how he could counteract any further questions if they were renewed. As far as this present mission was concerned any leakage of his identity was somewhat irrelevant, but it could affect his usefulness for future work in London where they both had to return.

He realized then that he was not completely happy about her, for despite the clearance from Smith's department it was not impossible for the department to slip up. Then he realized something else, for although Caroline claimed to have seen him several times during the past few days, he had not noticed her among the pack of press representatives who had followed the tour. So where had she been? It was unlikely that he could have missed seeing her, very unlikely, and he was suddenly sure that she must have lied about being present with the press party. But why had she lied? And if she was not on San Quito to represent the *London Mail* then why was she here?

Larren's awareness had diminished as the questions expanded in his mind, and then suddenly the sardonic voice of Sanchez cut in through his thoughts.

The Mexican said softly.

"Is it not time you began to pray,

senor. Your time is now finished."

Larren's body stiffened as he snapped back to reality, but Sanchez was relaxed and unthreatening in his chair, his lean mouth creased with faint amusement. And then Larren understood what the Mexican meant.

The wall clock had ticked quietly past the hour of midnight, the deadline that had been set for Rafael's assassination. From this moment on Larren was the prime target for voodoo vengeance.

10

The Bells of Hate

THE crowds were restless, waiting, thronging the streets beneath the harsh blue sky and the white glare of the morning sun. There were thousands of them, Spanish Americans, West Indians, Negroes and Whites, and every inter-mixture of colour and race. Some were quiet, while some talked loudly; some were Christian and some were heathen; some were rich but most were poor; but they were all restless, they were all waiting.

They lined every step of the Presidential route, vastly out-numbering the spaced blue uniforms of the English and native policemen who were there to hold them back. They wore their Sunday clothes, the men in white shirt-sleeves or dark suits, and the women in bright flowery dresses. The children were well-scrubbed and wide-eyed, and most of them carried small flags to wave. There were many union jacks, but very few of the more gaudy colours of Maraquilla. They were all curious and expectant, but somehow there was no real sense of festivity in the air. The appearances were there, but there was something else, dormant and silent beneath the surface. And they waited.

Caroline Brand could sense the undercurrent beneath the mixed sea of faces, and she felt a faint sense of nervousness as she waited for the parade to approach. She was standing with a small group of pressmen in the Plaza Santa Maria, close to the Catholic Church of St. Mary's where the parade was to end, and the whole of the Plaza was packed solidly with people. She was conscious of the heat and the mutter of voices, and of the silent ticking of the watch on her wrist, and then slowly she became aware of another factor that she had almost missed. There were more men than women in the crowd around her, and there were nowhere near as many children as there should have been. And then she began to sense that it was not exactly the parade for which they were waiting.

★ ★ ★

Simon Larren felt the same disquietening atmosphere as the cavalcade of cars moved slowly into the city on the first stage of the circular route. He was sitting beside Reb Hansen in a Daimler driven by Inspector Barrios, and immediately ahead was the Rolls Silver Cloud that carried Dominguez and Rafael. In the lead car that preceded the Rolls Carleton, the Deputy Governor, was seated beside the chauffeur driver, while Sam Friday and Sanchez Lorenzo leaned back discreetly in the rear seat. An efficient squad of motor-cycle mounted police cleared the way, while a smaller squad brought up the rear behind the remaining cars that carried a host of lesser officials and a scattering of military staff.

The formation had started from the villa Marola, and now moved down the long hill towards the centre of Aparicio. The crowds were thinly spread here, and their reaction was mostly curiosity with a weak spate of cheering. The mass became denser as they reached the Plaza Nationale and turned left up the broad, palm-lined Avenue Colon towards the Town Hall, but the cheering did not gain in volume. Those who did cheer shouted only for their own President Dominguez, and no one voiced the name of Rafael.

At the end of the Avenue was the wide Plaza Centrale, faced by the Town Hall and Administration offices, and the big central post office. Here there was a huge crowd gathered along the pavements, and around the large, cascading fountains in the centre of the square, and the sound of cheering began to swell. The children in the forefront waved their flags excitedly. Simon Larren watched the close-packed ranks of passing faces as the cars swung slowly right along the main King's Street, and still he was uneasy. He didn't quite know why, but half way down King's Street the answer suddenly fitted into place. It was in the crowd, there was no pressure in them, no pushing forward, and even in the faces of those that the parade was leaving behind there was still a faint sense of anticipation. It was as though they were still waiting.

Larren glanced sideways at Hansen, and saw that the American no longer adopted his lounging pose. Hansen's mouth was shut and his face was the texture of bleak granite beneath his short-cropped hair.

Larren said quietly. "I guess you sense it too?"

Hansen looked at him sharply, and then nodded.

"They're too damned negative," he

said. "I'd feel happier back in a Jap-infested fox-hole on Guadalcanal than I do right now."

They said no more, but their concentration doubled as the cars continued their crawling progress. Larren knew now that Mackenzie had been right, and that the parade should have been called off, but it was too late, and they had passed the point of no return.

The multitude of dark, black, and swarthy faces blocked every side as they neared the next turning at the end of King's Street. They passed the University of Aparicio, the Museum and the Public Library, where the crowds stretched high up the broad steps to each of the wide-fronted buildings with their columned façades, and here and there, from the highest part of the crowd, came sporadic boos for Jose Rafael. The cavalcade crept round the corner into the long stretch of Port Royal Street, and still they were only half way along the intended route.

The next half mile seemed to take an age, and Larren began to sweat a little in the close heat. The sun was climbing high to the noon-day position and its glare bounced back from every wall and window, and glinted in flashes of dazzle from the mirror-like surface of the Rolls ahead. Twice Larren smoothed his palms along his thighs to clear the moisture.

At last the cars reached the junction where Port Royal Street branched right again towards the Plaza Santa Maria, and here the voice of the crowd increased in volume. But there was a derisive sound to it now and the cheering was not sincere. And there were more mingled taunts and boos for Rafael.

Larren could see Maraquilla's President sitting stiff and upright in the car ahead, and he guessed that Rafael would be adopting a fixed, forced mask of a smile. Vicente Dominguez was twisting from side to side, his own smile weak and strained as he lifted his hand in greeting to each side in turn.

Larren saw no reason to smile at all, but he felt a growing sense of relief as they neared the Plaza Santa Maria and he saw the high cross above the church showing ahead. The hidden tensions in the crowd were obvious now, but he felt that nothing would happen once they reached the sanctuary of the church. And surely after this Dominguez would have the sense to have his guest driven at top speed straight for the airport.

They entered the Plaza, still at a slow walking pace, and one by one the fleet of cars drew up in a perfect line along the left side of the square. Here the cheering rose to drown the scattered boos, but again there was that note of derision, and as the sound of the car engines stopped, so the cheers died down, and a slow hush came over the crowd. The Holy Church of St Mary's was still a hundred yards away, blocking the end of a short approach street across the square.

Larren said grimly. "This could be it."

Hansen nodded. "That fox-hole seems safer every minute."

They got out of the car then, for this was the closest to the church that such a large number of vehicles could be parked. Inspector Barrios was with them as they moved towards the Presidential Rolls, and behind them the occupants of the other cars were slowly climbing out and closing up.

Rafael remained seated until there were enough men by the Rolls to provide a partial shield, and then the Rolls driver, who was Sir Basil Trafford's personal chauffeur, circled round the long, square-angled bonnet to open the door. Rafael climbed out stiffly, his face showing signs of strain, and then Dominguez came out behind him. Barrios automatically fell into step behind Dominguez's shoulder.

The party assembled, and Sanchez and Sam Friday closed in on each side of Rafael. Carleton was with them, and it was the Deputy Governor who led the way across the square. The motorcycle patrol continued to stay ahead, riding slowly in double file. The rest of the party followed in an orderly crowd. Among them was Rosemary Keene, her red hair even more noticeable as she was the only woman there. She walked with an army Major, the chief military representative, who had politely offered his arm.

Larren dropped back slightly with Hansen, and by unspoken agreement they separated and each moved to the edge of the party, Larren filtering to the right and Hansen to the left.

The silent sea of faces were impassive behind the constables who lined the edge of the pavements to hold them back, but every pair of eyes watched with close expectancy. Larren stared back at them, searching for the first hint of sudden danger. But there was nothing there except that curious watchfulness.

He realized then that there were very

few children here, although there had been plenty of them along the earlier stages of the route. Those that were evident no longer showed signs of excitement, but looked up at their elders with puzzled eyes. On impulse he stopped scanning the faces of the crowd, and stared into the closer faces of the policemen spaced along the way. He saw then that even the native constables had absorbed some of the aura of anticipation; some of them looked merely wary, but some were afraid.

The slowly walking party left the square, and there was practically no sound above the dull pacing of their feet and the low reverberations of the motor cycles in front. The broad steps leading up to the church doors were only fifty yards ahead, and the far flung shadow of the high cross lay like a pointing sword in the dusty street. A faint surge of movement went through the crowd, and Larren realized that for the first time they were pressing forward after the parade had passed.

The two lines of motor cycles parted on either side of the cross's shadow, and then drew to a halt facing the steps. Carleton and the two Presidents moved between them.

That was when Larren saw the mulatto.

It was unmistakably the face of the big half cast who had performed the voodoo execution on Doctor Midnight's orders, and Larren's unsmiling mouth compressed hard as he took a single step forward. Then he realized that the mulatto was too far back in the crowd to offer any practical threat, but that he was staring ahead as though gripped in some form of breathless trance. Larren followed his gaze, and saw that he was not watching the party leaders who had now reached the first step, but that his eyes were fixed upon the closed doors of the church.

Larren moved forward fast, pushing through the pack of officials, and as if some sixth sense had warned him Reb Hansen was suddenly at his side.

"What is it?" Hansen's tone was clipped and his right hand was already inside his jacket.

"The doors," Larren rapped tersely. "At the start of a service they should be open."

Hansen looked up, and then his gun appeared as he forced his way forward at Larren's side. Dominguez, Rafael and Carleton were poised three abreast on the fourth step of the steep flight and they were all beginning to relax. They had run the gauntlet and sanctuary was just ahead. And then with a sudden hideous crash of sound the bells pealed out.

The thunderous clamour rolled in a battering wave from above the church, clanging in crazy disorder that had neither rhythm or reason. It was simply sound, shocking and frightening in its terrible magnitude. It deafened the ears and screamed at their nerves, and in the same moment the heavy oak doors at the top of the steps were kicked violently open.

Larren was still too far back and so was Hansen, and the barrier of suddenly immobile bodies checked their progress. Two men appeared between the opened doors of the church and the submachine guns cradled in their arms opened up in a hateful fury that drowned even the bells.

Larren saw Sanchez Lorenzo hurl himself upon Rafael, but whether the Mexican was in time it was impossible to tell, for those in the forefront of the party were toppling like leaves before a bloody wind. Screams echoed and died in the struggling confusion, and within a matter of seconds the barrier of bodies that barred Larren's view was cut away.

The Smith & Wesson was already in Larren's hand, comparatively puny but better than nothing. Its ringing bark was echoed by a heavier crack from Hansen's sawn-off Colt. Again the two guns echoed, almost in unison, and barely noticeable among the chaos. But one of the assassins staggered in the same moment. He poised like a broken reed, awaiting the next puff of breeze that would sway his balance, and then he released his grip on his sub-machine gun and fell headlong down the steps.

Both the body and the weapon crashed the full distance, and a prone, blue-suited figure suddenly came to life among the fallen and squirmed frenziedly towards the gun. The black hand of Sam Friday closed over the clattering weapon as the second assassin turned and fled back into the safety of the church.

Larren and Hansen scrambled forward, but again they were stopped as pandemonium burst among the watching crowd behind them. They turned as the mob tore through the restraining ranks of the police and charged towards the stunned and demoralized group below the church steps. This was what they had really been waiting for, and now they surged forward on impulse, spurred on by the insane signalling of the bells.

Only Friday seemed unaware of the danger from behind. The big negro had reached his feet and his face was knotted by determination as he rushed up the steps in pursuit of the fleeing second assassin. The submachine gun was in his hands and there was murder in his heart, but before he could reach the top of the steps there came a shattering explosion that bowled him backwards.

The explosion also checked the crowd, and their charge was halted as they stopped to gape. Even Larren was stunned by this continuation of the nightmare, and he had to force himself to turn back to face the church. The explosion had taken place in the doorway, bringing half the surrounding walls crumpling around the entrance. Smoke and dust swirled above the bricks and rubble that spattered down the broad steps, and any entry into the church was effectively blocked.

The last handful of bricks bounced towards the street as the echoes of the blast died away, and Larren saw Friday sprawled at the foot of the steps. The negro still clung fast to the submachine gun and he was weakly trying to rise. And then a voice in the crowd began to spur the mob to attack again.

Larren faced the danger as the mob began its second move, for the pealing bells still made their mad music to drive the thousand-headed animal on. The agitators among them, undoubtedly including the mulatto, were barely needed.

However, the shock of the explosion had given the shaken police forces time to rally, and now the thin line of constables had reformed to face the mob. The motor cycle squad had left their machines and strung themselves in a line across the road, and each man had pulled his pistol from his hip. The front of the mob halted, but the uproar of a full-scale riot reached them from the main Plaza where they had left the cavalcade of cars.

Larren turned and hurried to the foot of the church steps. Hansen was ahead of him and he saw that Rosemary Keene, seemingly unharmed, was already kneeling over Rafael. The carnage was ghastly, and over half of the official party were either dead or wounded.

Larren stared down at the scene, and then saw that the seemingly impossible had happened. Either by a miracle, or by the dedication of their bodyguards, both Dominguez and Rafael were alive. Dominguez was wounded and there was blood staining the right side of his white shirt beneath his jacket, but Rafael looked to be unscathed.

Then Larren saw why. Sanchez Lorenzo had saved Rafael at the cost of a broken arm. While the quiet Inspector Barrios and Carleton had protected Dominguez at the cost of their lives.

San Quito's president was staring dumbly at the two dead men and repeating dully.

"They — they pushed in front of me. They saved my life. They pushed in front of me . . . they pushed in front of me . . . "

Larren gripped his arm, and shook him hard.

"Take it easy," he rapped. "Snap out of it!"

Dominguez looked up at him, somehow he had retained his dark glasses but behind them his eyes were shocked. He swayed unsteadily and then felt for the patch of red at his side.

Larren looked round and saw two more men on their feet. One was the army Major who had escorted Rosemary Keene. The other was a young Lieutenant who appeared to be with him. Sam Friday, his face covered with dust and blood was coming towards him, doggedly shaking his head.

A fusilade of gunshots sounded above the clanging of the all-drowning bells, and Larren spun sharply to see that the police had been forced to fire over the heads of the advancing crowd. And then he saw something else. There were leaping fingers of flame beyond the heads of the crowd, and a slow crackle of burning reached him together with frenzied cheers from the Plaza.

Hansen saw it too. He had helped Rafael and Sanchez to their feet, and now all those that were capable were standing.

Hansen said flatly.

"They've fired our cars back in the Plaza. We've got to get out of here."

"You are too damned right, Reb." Sanchez was white-faced but he held his automatic in his good hand. "This is one hell of a revolution."

Larren was in full agreement, but with the entrance to the church blocked and the mob barring the way ahead every route of escape seemed impossible. He looked round desperately for an alternative, but although there were streets leading off on either side they too were blocked with people. The ring of police were being forced to contract, and at any moment the sea of faces could sacrifice their leaders to the few guns of the motor cycle squad and charge.

And then there was a new sound, roaring with unexpected suddenness above the racket of the bells. The mob seemed to twist and panic, yelling hysterically as they melted into two halves. A troop lorry burst through the gap, driving at full pelt from the side street to their left, and then skidding to a halt inside the circle. Larren's gun lifted automatically, and then he saw that the lone driver wore a Police Inspector's uniform. The man leaned out of the cab and bellowed hoarsely.

"Get in the back! And for Christ's sake hurry!"

Those who could move needed no urging, and Rafael led the scramble into the back of the lorry. Larren helped Dominguez and the others followed at random. Hansen pushed Rosemary Keene up in front of him, and then stepped back.

"Quickly, man!" Larren rapped.

"You look after them," Hansen yelled. "I'll cover our friend in the cab."

The American ran for the front, and as he reached the running board he gave an urging yell, and the lorry started to move. Hansen tumbled in as it picked up speed. Their driver headed for the second side street opposite, ramming his foot down to crash his way through.

And then the mob broke.

In the same moment a slim figure with dark gold hair slipped through the breaking cordon of police. She screamed Larren's name and he recognized the desperately running figure of Caroline Brand.

11

Escape from Aparicio

"SIMON! *Simon!* SIMON!"

Even above the multitudinous voice of the mob and the ear-shattering tumult of the bells that still boomed out from the dust-shrouded church Caroline's screams rang hysterically clear. She had lost her camera somewhere in the confusion and the collar had been half torn from her white blouse. There was a vivid red scratch mark running the full length of her bare arm and her face was twisted with the stark anguish of fear.

"Simon! For God's sake wait."

She was almost in reach of the accelerating lorry, her body straining and her legs sprinting with terrified haste, and then she stumbled as she uttered that last pleading cry and fell forward with arms outstretched. Had she completed the fall there was nothing that could have saved her from being trampled by the on-rushing mob that swarmed behind her, but even as she pitched forward Simon Larren leaned over the tailboard of the retreating lorry and lunged forward to grip the wrist of her outflung hand. In the same second the vehicle's blunt bonnet ploughed like a mechanised battering ram through the scattering crowd that blocked its way.

The savage jerk as his grip locked almost tore Larren from the lorry, and it pulled the falling Caroline to her knees. For a moment she was dragged in the lorry's wake, her mouth open and shrieking aloud as the dusty road surface peeled off both stockings and skin, and her weight drew Larren even further from the lorry. His arm was almost wrenching from its socket and his free hand began to slip away from the corner post of the hood frame that held him fast. Then a massive arm locked around his waist and a thick voice grated.

"Hold her, man. Hold her!"

Larren gritted his teeth and then trusted himself to Sam Friday's anchoring bulk as he used both hands to haul Caroline Brand towards him. Her feet dragged for a moment as he took the strain, and then she was running madly again to keep pace with the lorry. The yelling mass of the mob that had parted in front of them immediately enfolded them again as they shot through, charging in full chase, and their leader was close enough to grab Caroline's free arm.

The man was a hefty West Indian with bristly hair and coal black skin, and he howled like an animal as he fought Larren in a hideous tug of war, with Caroline Brand as both the rope and the prize. He dug in his heels and for a second it seemed that Larren would have to either break his hold or be yanked out into the road, and then the spitting crack of an automatic sounded by Larren's ear. A red hole sprang as if by magic in the centre of the dusky forehead and the West Indian went flying backwards to vanish completely beneath the feet of his companions.

Relieved of the additional weight Larren hauled the now half senseless girl off her feet and over the edge of the tail board. The lorry was speeding dangerously at full pelt and the pursuing pack was falling swiftly behind, and for a moment Larren could only hold his burden on the point of balance. And then other hands were helping him and he recognized the army uniforms of the Major and his Lieutenant as they bundled the limp body into the safety of the lorry.

Larren was breathing harshly, but slowly he relaxed. The restraining arm left his waist and he turned to face Sam Friday. The big negro was grinning shakily through the smeared blood and dust that masked his face.

"That was a good catch, man. We

should go fishin' again. But who is she?"

"A friend of mine," Larren said. "I met her on the plane from London." He gripped the negro's shoulder for a moment and added heartfully. "Thanks, Sam."

He noticed Sanchez Lorenzo then, leaning pale-faced against the inside of the hood. The Mexican's left arm was limp, but he still held his automatic in his right hand, and Larren realized that it was Sanchez who had killed his opponent in the tug of war. He voiced his thanks again.

Sanchez smiled faintly. "My pleasure, senor." And for the moment it seemed that all traces of the hostility that was between them were forgotten.

Larren turned his attention to Caroline Brand. She sprawled in an undignified and helpless heap against the tailboard. Her skirt was rumpled high above knees that were soiled with blood and dirt beneath shredded stockings, and her throat and chest were working convulsively as she struggled to breathe. But, he thought thankfully, at least she was alive. He started to kneel towards her, and then the lorry took a sharp corner that made them all lurch and stagger. By the time he had regained his balance Rosemary Keene had pushed past him.

The redhead knelt and deftly adjusted the other girl's skirt, then she helped Caroline to sit up. She glanced at Larren.

"I'll look after her, there's no real damage done."

Larren nodded. He looked around the lorry and saw that Sanchez and Friday had positioned themselves on either side of the open back, and that Friday still had the sub-machine gun. They made an effective deterrent to any further attack. The two army men were standing in close support, while Rafael and the half dozen government officials surviving from the parade were seated around the lorry in shocked and still unbelieving silence. Vicente

Dominguez was on his feet, speaking through the communication slit that looked into the cab. Larren picked his way forward and joined him.

They had left the centre of Aparicio now, and the Police Inspector at the wheel was driving as fast as he dared through the dusty suburbs. There were few people in the streets, for most of the inhabitants had flocked to line the route of the parade, and for a moment they had a respite from danger. Larren could see little except the back and shoulders of the man who had saved all their lives, for the Inspector was concentrating grimly on the road ahead.

Larren said quietly. "Where are we going?"

Dominguez answered, his voice was strained but clear, and he had regained full control of himself now that the first shock had passed.

"The Inspector is trying to circle round and then approach Police Headquarters from the north side of the city. We may be able to avoid the biggest part of the crowds that way."

Larren's mouth tightened dubiously and he made no comment.

The lorry roared on, ignoring speed limits and road signs as it twisted through the back streets. Their driver never once turned his head, but Larren could see from the clean line of his jaw that he was very young, probably no more than twenty-six or seven. Reb Hansen was alert and watchful by his side.

They rounded a corner and ran slap into a roadblock.

Two large American taxis, a grey Dodge and a bright yellow Buick, had been turned over in the road. Hansen bellowed a warning and the Inspector braked hard. The lorry's bonnet hit the roof of the Dodge and caved it in, causing an outcry of triumphant shouting from the small mob behind the barrier. The Inspector swore and crashed his gears into reverse as the mob came swarming through the narrow gaps on either side of the street, and a fusilade of stones and bottles flew towards them. Then Hansen's colt cracked twice over the heads of the nearest pack, and the whole lot fell back as the lorry backed away. They made another little rush as it turned round, but stopped again when they saw the threatening figures of Sanchez and Friday. The mere presence of the submachine gun in the big negro's hands was enough, and they allowed the lorry to go on its way.

Larren said tightly. "What now, Inspector?"

The young man glanced back then, looking at Larren with blue eyes, which except for their hardness were almost identical to Caroline Brand's.

"We'll circle again," he said flatly. "And then I'll try and make another run into the centre."

Larren nodded, and said no more.

Dominguez said. "Thank you, Inspector — " He hesitated. "I am sorry, I have not yet asked your name?"

"It's Shaw." The policeman spoke without looking round. "Andy Shaw. I was supervising crowd control near the church when everything blew up. We had some troops with us to help out, and fortunately this lorry was left standing up one of the side streets. So — " He smiled briefly. "I grabbed it."

"Thank God that you did," said Dominguez simply. And then he coughed and Larren saw his hand move again to the ugly red patch at his side.

"Perhaps you'd better sit down," he suggested.

"No, it is not necessary." Dominguez was weak but determined. "It is only a flesh wound and not too serious."

Larren stared at him for a moment, and then his gaze returned to the communication slit, between the heads of Hansen and Shaw to the street through which they were passing. The position of the sun told him that they were again turning towards the centre of Aparicio, and almost certainly into more trouble. The booming of the church bells had at last faded and stopped, and the air was quiet and menacing. It was high noon and the sun blazed directly overhead.

They left the deserted streets behind and passed thickening groups of people. Some of them yelled abuse or hurled stones, but Shaw kept his foot down and the lorry rattled past without giving them much opportunity to do any damage. And then suddenly Shaw was forced to stamp on the brake as another roadblock appeared ahead. More cars had been overturned and set on fire, and this time there was a bigger noisier mob.

The mob leaders saw the lorry in the same moment that Shaw saw them, and immediately there was uproar. They flowed towards the reversing vehicle like a bursting wave, and a fusilade of shots shattered the hot air. Larren saw then that not only were many of these men armed, but that they wore the khaki uniforms of the San Quitan Army. He knew then that he had been right in suspecting the worst.

There were no half measures now, and Reb Hansen was firing back in deadly earnest. Both he and Shaw were keeping their heads low as the policeman struggled to get the lorry facing back the way that they had come, and Larren was able to thrust his own Smith & Wesson through the communication slit over their heads. He saw two of the leading attackers spin and fall as he backed up Hansen's fire, and then a burst from a sten gun tore the cab windscreen into a murderous hail of flying glass.

The lorry crashed out of control and slammed into a shop window in another nightmare of broken glass, and there it stalled, broadside across the street. Both Shaw and Hansen were hunched to one side and their arms upflung to protect their faces, and from this angle Larren was unable to get a shot at the yelling mob. He felt a moment of despair as he heard the note of lustful laughter that came into that many-throated voice of violence, but he had forgotten Sanchez and Friday.

The submachine gun in Friday's hands added its own masterful music to the surrounding orchestra of hate, with the waspish spitting of the Mexican's automatic punctuating the rhythm. The guns outside continued to chatter in return, shredding holes through the taut canvas of the lorry's hood, but except for Larren and Dominguez the other occupants had dived in a mass for the floor and mercifully no one was hit. Dominguez tried to move forward, but Larren gave him a disrespectful thrust that slammed him face down with the others out of harm's way. Then Larren began firing blindly through the tattered canvas. Outside, the front ranks of the mob broke in disorder.

In the cab Shaw struggled to recover

his shaken wits, and despite the bleeding from a dozen cuts he managed to restart the engine and back away from the smashed shop-front. Hansen was cursing roundly, and bleeding in almost as many places as Shaw, but he too had managed to protect his eyes and there was a savage pleasure in them as he raised the sawn-off Colt again and renewed covering fire.

The lorry reversed, and then Shaw swung the wheel and crashed through the gears as his foot thrust the accelerator to the floor. Larren stumbled forward over the huddled bodies in the back and joined Sanchez and Friday. However, the mob was still frantically scattering, and were far too demoralized by the abrupt appearance of Friday's sub-machine gun to even think of giving chase. There was no need for further shooting, and of that Larren was glad, for the last time that he had pulled the trigger of the Smith & Wesson it had uttered only an empty click.

He glanced round to check that

everyone was all right, and then swiftly reloaded the gun as the bouncing lorry sped back towards the outskirts of the city. When he had finished Sanchez held out his own automatic.

"I too am empty. Will you oblige, senor?"

Larren nodded and took the offered gun. Sanchez then dug his right hand into his left pocket, wincing for a second as the move disturbed his injured arm. He handed over a spare clip of bullets and said softly.

"That is the last, senor. I am afraid that I only carry one spare clip."

Larren smiled grimly. "That makes two of us." He glanced at Friday.

The negro grinned. "I still got two clips for my own gun, but — " He tapped the submachine sadly. "But this little honey is just about empty."

Larren said flatly. "Then it's about time we got out of Aparicio. We can't win many more gun battles." He returned the Mexican's automatic, and then made his way back towards

Dominguez. He was aware of Caroline Brand watching him from the floor, with Rosemary Keene crouching close beside her, but he had no time now for women.

Dominguez had heard Larren's last comments, and he sat up straight as Larren approached. He was still holding his side and his face was pained, but his voice was sharp.

"We cannot leave Aparicio, Mr Larren. I must get to somewhere where I can restore law and order. I owe a duty to my people."

Larren said bluntly. "You can serve them best by staying alive, and you won't do that by making another attempt to get into the city. Half of that last mob were soldiers from your own army, and if the army has mutinied then the situation is fully out of hand, and you won't stop it until they've had time to sweat out some of their enthusiasm and start to think."

Dominguez looked as though someone had twisted a knife in his wound. His face paled and he said feebly.

"The army cannot have completely mutinied. It can only be isolated units."

"Even so, you're still facing a full scale revolution." Larren spoke harshly to hammer the words home. "Your enemies are very highly organized. The fact that they were able to take over the church in the face of all Mackenzie's precautions must surely prove that. And those bells were not rung merely to signal the attack on us, but to prompt an uprising over the whole damn city. You've got to get out until things settle down."

"But — " Dominguez seemed incapable of thought. "But where?"

"To Caligas." Larren had the answer ready. "We're on the right side of the city for the road north, and provided that there are no barricades on the main roads out we can be at the army post there in an hour." He paused, and then added. "But that's gambling that the troops stationed at Caligas are loyal. How well can you trust their C.O.?"

Dominguez said angrily. "I would trust Colonel Oparto with my life."

Larren smiled bleakly. "That's exactly what I'm proposing."

He turned towards the cab, but then Jose Rafael interrupted abruptly.

"One moment. What about me? Now that San Quito has become an island of revolution I think that your first duty should be to get to the airport so that I can return to Maraquilla. It is too dangerous for me to stay here."

Larren looked at him slowly, and now he saw no more reason to stop his distaste for the man from showing in his tone.

"The airport is one of the first places that the rebels would want to capture," he said flatly. "Only a fool would want to rush there at this stage."

Then he turned away again, ignoring the look of compressed fury that came on to Rafael's face as he pressed close to the communication slit to speak to Shaw.

The young Police Inspector listened, and then nodded grimly.

"I agree with that," he said. "It's pretty obvious now that even if we could get near Police Headquarters, or anywhere else that offered refuge here, we'd only find the place under attack from the mob. Caligas is our best hope."

Hansen added solid support and then the lorry began to thrust forward as Shaw pressed more decisively on the accelerator. Larren watched the streets flashing past them and hoped that he had made the right decision.

12

The Battle of Bloodbath Ridge

THEY were lucky, for either by oversight or delay the rebels had failed to block off the north road out of Aparicio. The outer streets of the city were again all but deserted and they escaped without another shot being fired. There were some anxious moments, but once they reached open country they were able to relax as the lorry roared at full speed along the narrow, dusty road through flat scrub plains that climbed slowly to rolling hills and timberland around Caligas.

Shaw was still at the wheel when they reached the small township, and he drove through fast without stopping. Both he and Hansen had disregarded Larren's offer of a relief and claimed that the blood on their faces came only from flesh cuts made by the flying glass and that none went deep.

Larren watched the faces of the townspeople as the lorry rattled through the poorly surfaced streets. They stood in clusters to stare at the wildly driven vehicle with its empty windscreen and the red-smeared faces in the cab. But they made no move to interfere and their expressions were neither hostile nor friendly.

Immediately on leaving the town the high wire fence surrounding the barrack blocks of the army post appeared ahead, and two minutes later Shaw was braking before the pole barrier across the gateway. A sergeant of the guard came running, with two armed soldiers hurrying at his heels. Larren started to move but the Major from Dominguez's staff gestured him back and then swung down from the back of the lorry to explain briefly to the hastily saluting men. A moment later the pole was lifted, and the Major ran forward to ride the running board as Shaw drove on.

The concrete roadway ran between rows of the long drab huts that formed the barrack buildings, and then brought them into the large parade square. Here Shaw stopped the lorry before the C.O.'s office, and there was an ominous silence as he shut off the engine. They waited, and nothing happened, and it was then that Larren realized that the army post had an air of desolation. Apart from the guard detail he had not seen a single soldier.

Larren was worried then, and for a moment he feared that he had made the wrong decision and that they had driven into some kind of trap. But then there came the sudden clatter of boots on the concrete, and he saw an officer followed by an N.C.O. and half a dozen soldiers running towards them. The soldiers were armed and wary, but their weapons were not yet levelled.

The Major stepped down from the running board of the lorry and went to meet them. The approaching party stopped and their officer, a middle-aged Captain, saluted sharply. The Major answered the salute and demanded.

"Where is Colonel Oparto, your C.O.?

"Sir, the Colonel is not here. I am Captain Valdez, I am in command until he returns."

Larren, who was watching closely, sensed the movement that Dominguez made beside him. He pressed the President of San Quito down and warningly shook his head. He wanted to be sure of the situation before announcing the identity of the lorry's passengers. Shaw and Hansen were both getting down from the cab, and Valdez was eyeing them uncertainly. Then the Major reclaimed the Captain's attention.

"I am Major Zamora, attached to President Dominguez's staff. You will tell me please, what has happened to Colonel Oparto? And where are the troops who should be here at this post?"

Valdez hesitated a moment, and then

answered frankly.

"Sir, there is grave news. A revolt has taken place in Aparicio, and it is feared that President Dominguez is dead. There is much fighting in the capital and we have received news that a large force of rebels are also approaching the city. Colonel Oparto has mobilized the bulk of the troops here and is attempting to intercept this rebel force."

Zamora's face was strained as he listened, and it was clear that the words came as a shock. Then he recovered himself and squared his shoulders.

"Then you will be glad to know, Captain, that the senor President is still alive." He went on to explain more fully the happenings in Aparicio, and their own presence here in Caligas.

While the Major explained, Larren helped Dominguez to descend from the back of the lorry. The rest of the party followed more slowly behind them. Dominguez waved away Larren's support once he had reached the ground, and walked steadily to join Zamora.

Valdez snapped to attention again, saluting smartly. He said earnestly.

"Senor President, I am relieved to see that you are safe. But — " His face became anxious. "You are wounded."

"Thank you, Captain, but it can wait." Somehow Dominguez managed a tired smile of reassurance. "First you must tell me all that you know of this force of rebels, and of Colonel Oparto's intentions?"

Valdez nodded, clearing his throat with a jerky cough.

"But of course, Senor President. These rebels are estimated at between five and six hundred men. They appeared from the forests behind us, and the column was seen by some peasant farmers as it moved in a wide circle to avoid Caligas. They are now somewhere in the hills to the west and are marching directly towards Aparicio."

Valdez swallowed hard and then

213

continued. "The map shows only one straight route through those hills for an army that needs to move fast, and that is through the valley beneath the long rise that is called Bloodbath Ridge. That is the place that was named after the battle in 1870 when a large band of runaway slaves defended the ridge against Government troops."

Dominguez nodded. "I know it — and I do know San Quito's history."

"Of course, Senor President." Valdez looked uncomfortable. "But to continue. Colonel Oparto believes that if he can occupy this ridge before the rebels can get through the valley then he will be able to halt their progress. He has taken all of the two troop companies stationed here except for myself and a score of men."

"I see," murmured Dominguez gravely. He looked down at the parade ground for a moment, and then raised his head again to look into the Captain's face.

214

"Have you any news of the situation in Aparicio? Any radio reports?"

Valdez said soberly. "The radio station is in the hands of the rebels, that much is certain. Their broadcasts also claim that they are in control of the airport, and of most of Aparicio itself. They also claim that you are dead and that this is a complete victory for the Communist Party which is now in power. They have assumed full independence from Great Britain, and the broadcast says that they have appealed to Cuba, China, and the U.S.S.R. to prevent any outside interference. The statement adds that the uprising was necessary to prevent — "

Valdez stopped awkwardly.

Dominguez said dully. "Go on, Captain. I wish to hear it all."

Valdez repeated the jerky cough that cleared his throat, and then began again. "They say it was necessary to prevent your liaison with the Dictator of Maraquilla. They say that you planned a military alliance that would have made San Quito into another oppressed dictatorship if they had waited for independence while you were still President."

Jose Rafael ejected a hiss of anger as his name was mentioned and took a stiff step forwards. Then he realized the futility of making any protest and became still. Dominguez did not seem to have even heard the movement behind him.

"It is the kind of fabrication I should have expected," Dominguez said slowly. "But tell me, is there any news of Sir Basil Trafford?"

Valdez shook his head. "The broadcast did not even mention the Governor's name. It is impossible to guess at his fate."

There was a long moment of silence, which no one was willing to break. And then at last Dominguez made a decision. He said determinedly.

"There is nothing that I can do here. My only course is to join Colonel Oparto in the hills. If he is successful in routing this rebel force we can then march on Aparicio and attempt to restore order."

He turned then and faced Rafael.

"My friend, I am sorry that your visit should have to end in this manner, but all that I can suggest now is that you and your party remain with me. Captain Valdez has no men to spare, but if we can reach Colonel Oparto he may be able to provide you with an escort. Then as soon as we can find a safe airfield I will do my best to arrange a plane to take you back to Maraquilla."

Rafael said sourly. "It seems that I have no choice."

Dominguez looked at him for a moment, and then turned back to Valdez.

"Captain, as you can see, some of us require medical attention. Is there a Doctor on the post?"

Valdez shook his head. "I am sorry, but our Doctor has accompanied Colonel Oparto."

"Then we must manage without."

Dominguez shrugged as though it were of no importance and turned away. It was then that Caroline Brand pushed forward. Rosemary Keene had bandaged her damaged knees with handkerchiefs during the drive but she still limped awkwardly. However, her voice was calm as she said quietly.

"Senor President, I have had some nursing experience, enough to fix some temporary dressings if there is a surgery on the post."

Dominguez smiled. "Well thank you, Miss Brand. I'm sure that there is a surgery." He saw Valdez nod and continued. "Perhaps first you could see to the Mexican gentleman's arm, and then I'll allow you to patch the hole in my own hide."

Caroline smiled, and seemed completely unaware of Simon Larren as he regarded her with close interest. Larren had marked her appearance at the church as yet another dubious coincidence, even though it was the most obvious place for a press photographer to be, and now he was wondering where she had gained her nursing experience. They had talked a lot during their affair in London, but she had never mentioned it before.

★ ★ ★

When they left Caligas half an hour later they were still travelling in the lorry that had brought them from Aparicio, but now Zamora sat in the cab, while his aide, Lieutenant Delgado, handled the wheel. Shaw and Hansen had exchanged their places with reluctance, but it was clear that the rank tabs of the two officers would provide their best passport in getting through the outer ranks of Colonel Oparto's troops when they neared the battle area.

The party was smaller now, for all of the lesser officials had been left behind at Caligas. However, in Larren's opinion it was still one too many, for

Caroline Brand was still with them. She had convinced Dominguez that her medical skill might again come in useful. Larren was uneasy about her presence, for Caroline was proving a much different character to the wanton playgirl he had known in London, and he distrusted anyone who acted out of character. It meant that one side of her nature was false. The question was — which one?

He mused on the problem, and then decided that perhaps he was prejudging her too harshly. She had certainly made a neat job of Sanchez's arm, and of fixing a pad over the ragged bullet gash below Dominguez's ribs. She had helped Shaw and Hansen too, cleaning their faces and applying plaster strips and iodine to the maze of cuts. Even Friday had benefited, although once the muck and dust had been washed from his face he had proved to have suffered only one cut across the temple, probably from a fragment of flying brick.

No one showed any desire for conversation, and they sat mostly in silence as the lorry rattled along a gradually worsening road surface through increasingly hilly country. The silence gave Larren time to think, and Caroline Brand faded slowly from his mind as he began the more pressing assessment of their present position. It was grimly clear now that the fifth column of San Quito's Communists was even more powerful and organized than anyone had suspected, and with the newly-revived cult of voodoo to control by terror where their propaganda might fail they must have a near unbreakable grip on the mass of the island's population. It was possible that Dominguez could regain control if there were enough loyal officers like Oparto to stand by him, but Larren remembered the troops among the rioters in Aparicio and he was more than doubtful.

Larren's thoughts continued cheerless, and then suddenly they fled away and his mind became empty, and his senses alert. Hansen too had become tense, and they both recognized in the same moment the faint sounds of distant battle. The lorry continued at the same pace and the sounds grew clearer; a confusion of rifle and sten gun fire, swamped by the chatter of heavy machine guns. Larren could even pick out the lighter stutter of a Bren gun, and for a moment his mind held a vivid picture of the war-torn fields of Holland in 1944. It was a memory which most men had wanted to forget, but to Larren's hard lips it brought a fleeting smile of pleasure.

A moment later there was a shouted challenge from the road ahead, and the lorry braked violently to a stop. Larren listened as Zamora answered the challenge, but the words were in Spanish and he did not understand. There was a brief conversation between the Major and their challenger, and then the lorry drove on. They passed a small squad of San Quitan soldiers and Larren noted that they now had a guide clinging to the running board.

Dominguez said quietly. "They are Colonel Oparto's men, and we are now being taken direct to his temporary command post."

They drove on for another ten minutes, and although the sounds of shooting grew louder, they also became more sporadic, as though the battle had lulled or was over. They were challenged twice more, but their guide shouted an explanation and the uniforms of the Major and the Lieutenant in the cab were accepted as proof of their identity. The terrain was very rugged now, and too rolling to give an open view for any distance. They passed many struggling groups of soldiers, and Larren knew from their faces that if the battle had been won then it was most certainly not by Oparto's forces. The haggard look that slowly crept over Dominguez's face showed that he knew it, too, and Jose Rafael was looking definitely alarmed.

They came upon the command post quite suddenly. It was simply half a dozen canvas tents pitched in a low valley, surrounded by some two to three hundred battle-stained troops. Larren watched the men's faces as the lorry drove slowly between their ranks, and he knew that he was seeing a beaten army. Dominguez got to his feet and moved slowly to the back of the truck, staring almost in horror at the slack, sullen faces.

And suddenly there was a change. The pale, scholarly face behind the dark glasses was recognized and a stir of new life swept through the watching men. The word *President* and the name *Dominguez* passed from mouth to mouth as they pushed to their feet. A man shouted the name aloud and abruptly the murmur became a roar, a full-throated cheer of pleasure and approval. Dominguez slowly raised a hand, and then his face relaxed in a feeble smile. Simon Larren saw that Dominguez's weak eyes were moist

224

behind his protecting glasses, and he knew then that as long as Vicente Dominguez lived there was always hope for San Quito.

The lorry stopped beside the tents and Dominguez scrambled quickly down. Larren and Shaw followed after him, but Rafael and his bodyguards stayed in the lorry with the two women. The mass of soldiers were still yelling lustily, and Dominguez stood and faced them with his hand raised and smiling his simple smile of appreciation until one of the tent flaps opened and the flustered figure of Colonel Oparto appeared.

"Senor President! Praise be to God it is really you!" The Colonel was as delighted as his men as he hurried forward, and he seized Dominguez's hand and wrung it warmly.

Dominguez found another tired smile and said.

"Thank you, Colonel. It is good to know that I am again among loyal friends. But tell me please, what has been happening here?"

Oparto hesitated, his lined face suddenly wretched with failure. Then he said bitterly. "I have bad news, Senor President. But perhaps you had best come inside."

Dominguez nodded slowly, and then he passed through the tent flap which Oparto held open for him. Shaw hesitated, but Larren followed the Colonel into the tent and the policeman finally made up his mind to accompany them. Zamora and Delgado entered quietly behind him.

Four of Oparto's staff officers were already inside the tent, waiting around a large desk-table on which a large scale map of the area was pinned open. There was a brief moment of introductions as Dominguez acknowledged the four officers, and Larren noticed that like their Colonel they all showed signs of strain and battle-wear. Oparto finally picked up a pointer and indicated the map.

He said slowly. "As you can see,

Senor President this hill, which is known as Bloodbath Ridge, is the highest point in the area, and it overlooks this valley which provides the most direct route through these hills. I hoped to occupy that ridge, and from there scatter the rebel forces approaching Aparicio. Unfortunately, the rebels had occupied the ridge when I arrived, so that now they hold the best position. We have tried to take the ridge, but they have six heavy machine guns strung across the top of the hill which have caused slaughter among our troops. We have been forced to fall back." He stopped, and then said dully. "Too many of our men were cut down in this first battle, and those that remain will not face the ridge again."

There was a stillness in the large tent, and even the soldiers outside had quietened now. Dominguez's face had gone a little paler and at last he said.

"Then what do you propose to do, Colonel?"

Oparto faltered, and then said unwillingly. "There is only one thing that I can do, and that is to wait here and engage the enemy when they leave the ridge. They cannot stay there for ever."

Dominguez stared into the Colonel's face. "But that means that the battle remains static, and I need your troops to return to Aparicio."

"And I would gladly follow you, Senor President." Oparto spoke earnestly, spreading his hands in a gesture of supplication. "But to turn our backs on our present enemy invites disaster. I must destroy them first."

"Then we cannot wait until they come to us. We must take that ridge!"

"But the men will not face the ridge again," Oparto was almost crying with despair. "They say it is suicide to try."

Dominguez was silent for a moment, and then, despite the paleness his face took on a new grimness of expression. He said quietly.

"You saw the reception they gave me as I drove in. I think — I think that if I were to personally lead them then they will follow."

There was a shocked, horrified silence, and then the outburst.

"No," Oparto cried. "That would he madness. I would not allow it."

"No, Senor President. No!"

"You cannot do this. You must reconsider."

"If you die, then all is lost," Oparto insisted. "I will not allow it!"

Dominguez seemed to recoil for a moment, and then anger flooded through him and his fist crashed down hard on the table. The gesture was so unexpected, so alien to the quiet, learned character of the man, that it brought him instant silence.

He stared around the ring of stunned faces, and then said harshly. "None of us are of any use to San Quito if we simply sit here on our backsides while our enemies laugh at us from the hill-top, while their allies strengthen their grip on Aparicio. We must act, and we must scatter these rebels who oppose us here. We must take that ridge. I believe that for me the men will fight, and if that is so, then I will lead them!"

"But you are a politician, not a soldier," Oparto pleaded. "It does not matter," Dominguez shouted at him. "You will inform your men, Colonel, that we will make a second attack on Bloodbath Ridge one hour before dawn. And you will tell them I shall be leading them."

Oparto looked into the President's face and saw the determination that was written there, and very slowly he nodded.

* * *

Simon Larren watched from the background, hard-eyed and unsmiling. He knew that nothing would deter Dominguez from leading the next attack, for the disillusioned President felt that he personally had plunged his country into the present wave of warfare, and that only he could lead them out. Larren also knew that if Dominguez were to be killed then there would be no hope for a peaceful settlement on San Quito. For even if Britain sent troops to quieten her island Colony there would be no one to take the President's place, and martial law could only bring further discontent.

Larren decided then that his given task of protecting Jose Rafael was of secondary importance now, for the man himself was irrelevant now that the outbreak of violence that might have accompanied his assassination had already taken place. Clearly the man of prime importance now was Dominguez, and Larren didn't need fresh instructions to know that Smith and Whitehall would want San Quito's President protected at all costs.

The faint smile of pleasure appeared again on Larren's lips, and a light began to gleam in his eyes. The men who had trained him had called them killer's eyes, and they reflected his decision to take a hand in the battle of Bloodbath Ridge.

13

Dawn Attack

SEVEN hours later, and in pitch darkness, Simon Larren lay perfectly still in a slight hollow at the foot of the rebel-occupied ridge. He was now wearing dark green trousers, shirt and battle blouse, all army issue provided by Colonel Oparto which would help him to blend into the grassy slope. However, he still wore his own rubber-soled shoes, knowing that they would be more silent than nailed boots if he were to encounter any rocky ground. A loose cord around his neck secured a borrowed army revolver, a 45 with more kick than his own Smith & Wesson 38, which nestled snugly between his shoulder blades beneath the blouse. In that position it could not possibly make any betraying clink against a rock or stone. In his right hand he gripped his knife, the only weapon he hoped it would be necessary to use until he was in position, while hooked to the back of his belt were two four inch Mills bombs.

The keen blade of the knife had been carefully dulled so that it could not glitter, and Larren's face, the backs of his hands and the back of his neck had been thoroughly blackened. He had been especially careful about the back of his neck, for one of his fellow agents in S.O.E. had died through forgetting the faint white blur revealed above his collar when he tucked his face close into the ground. The top of the man's spinal column had been neatly severed by a well aimed bullet from a German sentry. All that was long ago now, and the Special Operations Executive had finished with the war, but it was Larren's long memory that helped to keep him alive.

Now he gazed up the black slope of

the ridge, searching for the unseen men, and the six lethally-placed machine gun nests which he knew were strung out above him. One, with luck two, of those machine guns, were the target of his one-man mission. The defensive fire from one flank of the ridge would have to be reduced if Vicente Dominguez was to lead the dawn attack and live.

There had been a flurry of protest from Oparto and his fellow officers when Larren had announced his intention of taking part in the battle, but it had gradually died. Larren had pointed out that for one trained and experienced man acting alone it would not be impossible to scale Bloodbath Ridge at night, and that their only hope for success was for someone to knock a hole in that line of machine guns as the battle started. Dominguez had listened to the argument in silence, but he knew fully Larren's position and background, and when he had at last spoken it was to accept Larren's offer.

There had been a final plea from

the younger officers, claiming that if the job was possible then one of them should be allowed to attempt it, but Larren had again stressed that he was best fitted for the task. He had also refused the offer of a squad of men, stating flatly that only stealth could get him to the ridge-top and that any company would only be an added danger. Just two grenades, if thrown accurately, could knock out two gun-pits, and all that was necessary was to get into position. He had then told Dominguez to lead his attack against the west flank of the ridge, and Dominguez had agreed.

Now Larren began to inch his way slowly up the slope.

He had memorised every detail of the large field map on the table in Oparto's command post, and he had thoroughly studied the ridge itself through borrowed field glasses during the last hour of fading daylight, so that now he was fully confident of his knowledge of the terrain. He was approaching from the western end of the ridge almost directly beneath the first of the six machine guns. He had plenty of time, and for the moment the maintenance of complete silence was his only concern.

It was a cloudy night, for the most part obscuring the moon, and for that he was grateful. During the moments when the moon did gleam palely through the ragged gaps in the cloud bank, he simply relaxed and lay still, merging like a human chameleon into the long grass. His ears probed the darkness, but there was nothing to alarm him.

It took Larren an hour to reach a clump of boulders which he knew to be half way up the hillside. Here he relaxed for a long time and listened. He could hear the murmur of voices now, and the occasional clink of boots or tin mugs along the crest of the ridge. Once or twice he detected the red glow of cigarettes, but he guessed that the bulk of the rebels would be encamped on the far side of the ridge. Only the lookouts, and those necessary to man the gun-pits would be guarding the firing line.

Quietly Larren made himself comfortable, and then he remained in his covering position for the next hour. His limbs were relaxed except for the brief moments when he stretched and flexed his muscles to keep them free from cramp, but his senses were constantly alert. At the end of the hour there had been nothing to disturb him, and he felt reasonably satisfied that there was no risk of encountering any rebel patrols along the face of the slope. He was also sure that there were no sentries below the line of machine guns, and that was going to prove a bad blunder for the rebels. He guessed that their leaders had little practical military experience, and that it was only by chance that they had beaten Oparto's troops to the best defensive position.

He began to move again, still

without hurry, and still concentrating on remaining absolutely soundless. His breathing was regular and even, and like a gradually lengthening shadow he drew away from the clump of rocks.

He was genuinely enjoying this stealthy approach in the night. Silence and darkness had always been his fondest allies, and there was a supreme satisfaction in being completely dependent upon his own courage and skill. And the greater the odds against him, the greater the satisfaction. It was this ability to actually take pleasure from these conditions, and even lust for the swift knife thrust and the dead sentry that so often marked the end, that had made him invaluable to S.O.E., and then, much later, invaluable again to Smith and Counter-espionage.

He was very near to the crest of the ridge now, and he lay still once more until he had definitely placed the position of the first machine gun. It was some thirty yards above him, and he listened until he had distinguished the occasional mutter of sound into three separate voices. He decided then that three would be the standard team; one gunner, one man to handle the ammunition belt, and a third to cover their backs from any unexpected attack. The pattern would be repeated in the other five gun pits spread at fifty yard intervals along the ridge, and he knew from his binocular survey earlier that there were Bren gunners in between.

Carefully he moved to the left, exercising every caution. The knife was between his teeth, and his free hand gently searched every inch of the ground ahead for any loose stones that might dislodge and rattle. When he found one he lifted it clear and placed it delicately to one side. After ten yards, that took twice as many minutes, he began to move at a tangent, still moving left, but slanting again towards the ridge top. The voices of the rebel forces were very clear, conversing quietly behind the line of the ridge. More cigarettes glowed, and there were more unexplained clinks and clatters.

Larren was on the far western end of the ridge now, and as he expected he found sentries above him. There were two of them, standing close together with sten guns slung from their shoulders. Larren froze silently against the hillside, and waited until he was sure they were alone.

When he was satisfied he carefully peeled back his shirt cuff, shielding his wristwatch as he revealed the luminous dial. He had two hours before dawn, and one hour before Dominguez launched his attack.

Calmly he waited. He was in a striking position, and there was no need to move any farther until the time came for action.

Half an hour later the two sentries above him separated, the faint silhouette of their forms parting on the ridge top. One of them became obscured by the blackness of the ridge, and from that and the shuffling sound of his progress Larren knew that the man was coming towards his hiding place. He tensed, but he did not panic, for he knew that he had made no sound or movement that could have possibly been detected. Then he heard the man stop and fumble with his clothes, and he understood.

For a moment Larren hesitated, but it was unlikely that anyone would check the guard in the next thirty minutes before the scheduled attack, and as those two sentries were in his way it would be criminal to miss such an opportunity. He heard the sound of the sentry relieving his bladder, and carefully he rose to his feet and padded forward. He saw the man's back in the gloom, and closed the last three yards in two silent strides. His hand fastened on the man's mouth, drawing back his head, and the knife point thrust neatly behind the windpipe and severed outwards. It was a lesson in efficiency and the luckless wretch was dead without a struggle.

Gently Larren lowered the body, and then he transferred the man's cap to his own head and the sten gun to his own shoulder. Then his lips murmured softly.

"You shouldn't have been so shy, you were safe with your comrade."

He smiled sadly, and then walked boldly up the ridge. When he came in sight the second sentry waited for him unsuspecting, for with the peaked cap and the snout of the sten sticking above his shoulder Larren's silhouette was identical to the man's dead companion.

The man spoke softly in Spanish, a casual question.

Larren grunted and shrugged his shoulders as he walked past.

The puzzled sentry started to turn, and then Larren spun swiftly on one heel. His hand clamped on the man's mouth, the head came back, and the knife made its well-trained movement.

Simon Larren was now in technical command of this end of the ridge, almost within throwing distance of the first gun-pit. His watch said twenty-five minutes before the attack and he was very confident.

★ ★ ★

The ultimate attack on Bloodbath Ridge came exactly on time. The darkness had become less absolute, more the filtering greyness of pre-dawn, and Larren could vaguely distinguish the terrain close around him. The nearest machine gun nest was still just a little too far to his right for him to see its outline, but the muttered sounds of the men who manned it had enabled him to accurately mark its position. He still wore the cap and the sten gun that gave him the silhouette of the sentry he had killed, but now his knife was thrust into his belt and he had brought the borrowed army revolver round to the front of his waistband where it would be swiftly accessible. He had unhooked the two grenades, and these now lay tidily at his feet. He was standing bolt upright.

He heard the first faint movements of Dominguez and Oparto's men at the foot of the ridge, and his muscles began to tense. Then he forced them to relax. The vague sensation of movement would be hardly noticeable to anyone who did not know exactly when to expect it. He listened closely, and although he knew that the San Quitan troops must be inching forward he could hear nothing more.

Then abruptly there was a clink of metal on stone, silence, and then a whisper of grass. They were still at the foot of the slope but surely those machine gunners must have heard. The night was still pitch black at the foot of the valley, and from the blackness there came again the whisper of disturbed grass, a whisper that was repeated all along the face of the ridge. *Surely they must hear now?*

Larren realized suddenly that his palms were sweating, and he dried them carefully along his thighs.

He heard the muffled movements again, and knew that the men below him could not remain undetected for many seconds longer. He reached down and picked up one of the grenades in his left hand, and he could feel his heart hammering like a voodoo drum. There was another clink of steel from below, and then abruptly there was a ringing cry of alarm from one of the sentries along the ridge top.

The night erupted into a shattering nightmare of sound. Every gun that defended the ridge seemed to open up in the same moment and there was a hideous crash of fire. The troops below answered the hail of death with their own automatic weapons and all was chaos and confusion.

Simon Larren was already whirling into action. He threw aside the hampering sten gun and scooped up his second grenade as he sprinted blindly forward along the ridge. The first machine gun was clearly marked by the flashes of flame spurting from its muzzle, and Larren had eyes for nothing else as his teeth wrenched the pin from the grenade in his right hand. He ran another ten yards and hurled the bomb so that it landed just on the edge of the sand-bagged gun pit. Then he dived flat.

The grenade blasted on impact, the sound wave and its disintegrating splinters tearing through earth and air. Larren was bounding to his feet before the debris stopped falling, and the pin of the second grenade was already yielding to his teeth.

He dashed to the edge of the first gun pit, where one dead and two badly stunned men were sprawling around the abruptly-silent gun, and then with all his strength he hurled the second grenade at the next machine-gun.

He didn't wait to see it land but sprang down into the first gun pit with the army revolver almost leaping into his hand. The two survivors of the gun crew were struggling upright and one was attempting to aim a rifle as Larren fired twice. The kick of the heavy 45 slammed them both back into the dirt, stilled for ever.

The second grenade hit down and exploded short of its target but it gave Larren a moment's cover as he scrambled into position behind the first gun. He had deliberately avoided what could have been a direct hit with his first grenade, and now he saw thankfully that the gun was not buckled. He pivoted the barrel to face along the ridge top and mercilessly raked the remaining defensive positions.

The next five minutes were sharp and furious as death sang its screaming chorus of sound along Bloodbath Ridge. The stabs of flame from the next gun pit ended abruptly in Larren's first burst of fire, and from then on he kept the rebels at bay as the loyal San Quito troops rushed up the practically undefended slope behind him. The chattering machine gun eventually jammed as was inevitable without another man to feed the ammunition belt, but by then Vicente Dominguez was leading his men over the crest of the ridge.

Larren sat back on his heels behind the jammed gun as his allies swept past to complete the routing of the demoralized rebels, and he forced his still accelerating heart to relax. He was breathing heavily, but the savage light was beginning to fade from his grey-green eyes, and he felt that he had done enough.

14

Into the Swamp

THE dawn was well established as Larren returned to Oparto's command post, and the sky glowed the colour of red rose petals along the skyline of the eastern hills. There were still isolated bursts of gunfire coming from the ridge behind him, but the main rebel forces were in full retreat and he had left the mopping-up operations to Dominguez and Oparto at the head of their troops. He was somewhat surprised to find that despite all the lethal ironmongery that had whistled around him during the battle he was still unscathed, and decided that for once he was leading a charmed life. On his last major assignment, which had taken him into the Arctic seas beyond Norway, he had been shot twice, so perhaps this was his turn to be lucky.

He reached the temporary head-quarters of canvas, and saw that there were now only a dozen soldiers there, left no doubt for the protection of Rafael. He tried to avoid the tent that had been placed at the disposal of the President of Maraquilla and his party, hoping to slip back into the Colonel's tent where he had previously changed his clothes, but the chatter of comment from the soldiers betrayed his arrival. The flap of the guest tent was pushed open and Caroline Brand appeared. Her face was anxious as she hurried forward, and the first rays of sunrise enhanced the dark gold beauty of her hair as she limped to meet him.

"Simon!" she cried thankfully. "Oh, Simon, I'm so glad to see you. Major Zamora told us what you were going to do."

She stumbled awkwardly as she reached him and he gripped her shoulders with both hands to steady her. For a moment her breasts pressed against his chest, and he was suddenly certain that whatever else she might be her present relief was very real. He could feel it in the faint trembling that passed through her body, and see it in the shining blue of her eyes. He smiled and said softly.

"It's all right, Caroline. I did what I set out to do. I'm still alive. And the battle is won."

She still looked up at him, and her red lips parted in a shaky smile. On a sudden impulse he inclined his head and kissed her, seeing her eyes widen and then close.

"That," he said. "Is indisputable proof that I'm alive."

Her smile became more relaxed, but before she could answer the curt voice of Jose Rafael bit into their private world.

"Larren, what the hell have you been playing at? Have you forgotten that I, and not the stupid battles of San Quito, should have been your first concern?"

Larren turned slowly to see the angry arrogance of the dictator's thin face. Rafael stood just before the tent and the formidable trio of Hansen, Sanchez and Friday was, as always, behind him. The three bodyguards were deadpan, their faces devoid of expression.

Larren took a step forward and said brutally. "You've got your priorities mixed, Rafael. Surely even you can see that the reasons for keeping you alive are no longer valid."

Rafael's face threatened to explode, and Larren could see the flush of blood rising in his thin cheeks. The dictator stood for a moment, and then spun on his heel, thrusting savagely between Sanchez and Friday as he returned to his tent. The big negro hesitated a moment, and then followed his employer. Sanchez clenched his teeth against the pain that had come from his wounded arm as Rafael had knocked against it, and then he too turned into the tent.

Larren watched them go, and then

started to move away towards Oparto's tent. He had to pass close to Reb Hansen, and the tall American moved casually into his path. Larren stopped, meeting Hansen's eyes. The man's face looked somewhat battered with its iodine-dabbed cuts and strips of plaster, but the grey eyes were still bleak beneath the short-cropped hair. Then Hansen smiled.

"You should have told me what you were up to," he said quietly. "I would have given you a hand. I haven't played those games since Guadalcanal."

Larren stared, momentarily uncertain, and then he realized that Hansen meant what he had said. He relaxed then, and returned the smile.

"I'll remember that, Reb. But I'm hoping that that was the one and only time that those games will be necessary."

Hansen shrugged. "So long as you know." And then he turned aside and went to join his colleagues.

Larren walked thoughtfully to Oparto's

tent and went inside. He changed back into his own clothes and then sat down on the Colonel's camp bed. He had done a lot of wondering about Caroline Brand, and now he was also beginning to wonder about Reb Hansen.

★ ★ ★

It was twenty minutes later that Simon Larren became aware that something had gone badly wrong. The troop lorries were returning too soon from the ridge and the hub-bub of confusion that had started to grow outside the tent was too agitated, and the voices too sharp and frightened for an army that should have returned victorious. He got up and went outside, and saw a chaos of men and trucks spilling around the camp, and from the direction of the ridge more lorries and men on foot were hurrying away from the scene of the battle. Some of the running men were even empty handed, as though they had thrown aside their weapons in order to accelerate their escape. The scene told its own unmistakeable story, that the San Quitan troops had been routed.

For a moment it seemed impossible that the certain victory he had left behind could have turned into this disorganized retreat, and then he accepted the evidence of his own eyes. He ran forward and grabbed the arm of the nearest N.C.O. and demanded harshly.

"What happened back there? Where are your officers?"

The man twisted, his face angry, and babbled something in Spanish that was too fast for Larren to understand. Larren swore, and then he saw that the two staff officers who had accompanied the lorry from Aparicio had appeared from one of the tents, and that Major Zamora was questioning a group of reluctant soldiers. Larren pushed the N.C.O. away and ran to join the Major. Hansen appeared in the same moment, and so did Andy Shaw, the Police Inspector.

Zamora faced them, and his tired face was creased with lines of bitterness. He said wearily.

"Gentlemen, it is terrible news. The battle was all but over when a column of rebel reinforcements fell upon our troops as they chased the defenders from the ridge. They must have approached during darkness and their presence was a complete surprise. Everything is now in disorder."

Larren stared at him, still unwilling to believe, and then he said flatly. "What's happened to Dominguez?"

Zamora hesitated, and it was obvious that he did not know. He turned to question the defeated troops again, and then stopped as the sound of a fast-approaching jeep grew in volume from the direction of the ridge. Automatically every head was turned towards the sound and they saw the vehicle bouncing crazily over the grassy terrain towards them. There were more lorries behind and more men fleeing on foot.

Zamora said hopefully. "Perhaps this

is the President." They waited in silence for the jeep to come near, and Larren barely noticed that Rafael had appeared again. The dictator's remaining two bodyguards were at his heels, and Rosemary Keene was holding on to his arm. They were all looking ill at ease. Caroline Brand came and stood by Larren's side.

The jeep screeched to a stop, its wheels slithering sideways on the wet grass as the brakes were applied, and two men scrambled hastily out. They both looked dirty and desperate. One Larren recognized as one of Oparto's field officers, and the other, much to his relief, was Vicente Dominguez. The President staggered a little as he left the jeep, and the red stains beneath his open coat showed that his wound had re-opened. However, Larren sensed that the tears in the man's eyes were not due to any physical pain.

Caroline Brand moved forward to help him, but Dominguez waved her away. He stood for a moment, facing them in silence, his face marked with anguish, and then he said desolately.

"All is lost. We won the ridge, but the rebels had reinforcements who counter-attacked as we tried to follow up our brief victory. Colonel Oparto is dead, and our troops — those that have survived — are deserting by the dozen." He paused, and then spoke the final blow. "The reinforcements were troops of my own army — from a post farther north where three full companies were stationed — their officers must have sold out to the Communists."

The new hopelessness of their situation lay like a pall of stillness around the handful of canvas tents, and then Rafael pushed forward and asked harshly.

"So what happens now? What do we do?"

Dominguez said bluntly. "We do the only thing possible. We take flight. Around us on three sides are the rebels, but to the east lies an area of swamp and jungle that will hide us easily if we can but reach it. From

259

there I do not know, but that we can decide later. The important thing is to get away from here as quickly as possible before we are captured."

Rafael's thin reserve of patience burst in a fury of words, and for a moment he was almost incoherent as he cursed the folly that had brought him to San Quito. He raved at Dominguez, blaspheming wildly, and finished by refusing flatly to skulk like a criminal through a swamp.

Dominguez waited for him to finish, and then said bluntly.

"Senor Rafael, you may come with me, or take your chances with my enemies. I can offer you no other alternative." And then he ignored the fuming President of Maraquilla and turned to address Zamora.

"Major, will you arrange, if possible, for a dozen soldiers to accompany us. You and Lieutenant Delgado can place yourselves at the disposal of Colonel Oparto's successor, or join us if you think fit."

Zamora said promptly. "Our duty is plain, Senor President, we shall go with you."

Dominguez glanced round the remaining faces.

Larren said. "Consider me as a replacement for Inspector Barrios."

Andy Shaw smiled grimly. "Commissioner Mackenzie would have my hide if I didn't echo that."

Dominguez looked expectantly at Rafael. The dictator flushed and then snapped.

"Damn you! You know I have no real choice."

Dominguez smiled then, and as he turned away he held his hand towards Caroline Brand in a tired gesture of gallantry. "And you will stay with us also I hope. I need my nurse to repair my hide."

Caroline smiled and moved to help him.

★ ★ ★

They left the scene of the battle as swiftly as possible, for with fresh rebel troops liable to appear at any moment it was too dangerous to delay. Zamora had commandeered two lorries and he and his Lieutenant again manned the cab of the lead vehicle carrying the Presidential party. While in the following lorry rode a dozen loyal soldiers under a sergeant, whom the Major had hastily assembled to form an escort.

They bounced wildly and at full speed over the uneven ground, and almost immediately the hills began to level out into flatter but more wooded country. In twenty minutes they were clear of the hills altogether, and scrub, bushes, and clumps of trees were all around them. Lieutenant Delgado, who was once more fighting the wheel, was forced to slow down in order to pick his way across the increasingly difficult terrain. The tangles of trees and undergrowth became larger, linking gradually together until at last it was impossible to find a way through. Delgado stopped the lorry, leaving it balanced at an angle on a tangled slope, and switched off the engine. From there on they abandoned the lorries and continued on foot.

Rafael made another protest as he descended to the ground, but even though there had been no pursuit it would have been folly to have stayed in the open where the rebels swarmed the hills, and so he had been ignored. Zamora sent his sergeant ahead with a party of men to cut a path with their bayonets, and the rest of the party plunged behind them into the jungle of tall trees and giant fern.

The mass of vegetation and creeping vine that choked the boles of the trees became denser as they progressed, and soon each one of them was perspiring heavily. The branches above had almost shut out the sun, but nothing could shut out the steamy heat. Dominguez was feeling the pain of his wound, even though Caroline had readjusted his bandages as well as she was able before they had started, and Larren and Zamora walked on either side to give him support. Directly behind them Andy Shaw was helping Caroline, for she was still half crippled from the ordeal of being dragged through the streets of Aparicio. Rafael, flanked by Rosemary Keene and his shadows, came next. While the young Lieutenant Delgado brought up the rear with the remainder of their escort.

They struggled on for another hour, and then the ground beneath their feet became ominously more spongy. The shape of the trees began to change, and the great gnarled roots of mangroves became more and more in evidence. The atmosphere became damper, and more gloomy, and there was the smell of moss and slime. The air tasted fetid and unhealthy, and the two women began to cast nervous glances at the rope-like curtains of bare vines.

Their steps began to squelch, and Larren could feel the mud sucking at the soles of his shoes each time he lifted them up. Then abruptly there came a splash and a muffled curse as one of the soldiers stumbled into a black pool. They moved on, more slowly now as those in the lead tried to pick a dry path. However, the patches of dry sod became fewer, until at last they were all wading into filthy black water that splashed around their knees.

For the rest of that day they struggled stolidly through the swamp, hampered by vines and tangled roots that spread from the feet of the squat mangroves. They were in water more often than they were out of it, and all of them kept a wary lookout for snakes or crocodiles. Once the water level rose to their hips, and the soldiers of their escort were forced to walk with their rifles or stens held above their heads. Larren pulled his Smith & Wesson clear to hold it above the water, and in the same moment he glanced back to ensure that the rest of the party had not fallen back. Caroline Brand was immediately behind him with Shaw, and he caught the moment of hesitation as her hand seemed to linger at the waist of her skirt, and then come swiftly away. He turned back as though he had not noticed the gesture, but his eyes had narrowed thoughtfully.

They were all tiring, and Dominguez was becoming noticeably weaker. Zamora was panting hoarsely and an hour before darkness he called a halt. Their escort searched around until they found a spot of rising ground where they could spend the night in comparative dryness, and they all moved wearily towards it. They were deep into the swamp now, and safe from any immediate pursuit, and somehow the sergeant and his escort detail found enough dry sticks to form a smoking fire.

They had only the water bottles and the field rations that the soldiers carried in the packs on their backs, but most of them were too tired to eat. Zamora instructed the sergeant to post a guard, and the rest of the soldiers formed a group a little way away from the fire. Rafael stared sullenly into the flames, while Rosemary Keene sat close beside him. However, the redhead was not quite close enough to actually touch him, and it was clear that the shine of being a dictator's mistress was fast rubbing away.

Caroline Brand knelt for a long while beside Dominguez, doing her best to clean and bandage his wound with Shaw's help. Then she left him to tend Sanchez's arm, and the Mexican smiled at her gratefully. Finally she stood up, and glanced around the poorly lit camp site until she encountered Simon Larren's watching gaze.

She moved slowly to where he lounged full length on the ground, propped on one elbow well clear of the fire. She lowered herself carefully because of her bandaged knees and sat down beside him.

He said quietly "How's Dominguez?"

"He should be all right," she said

doubtfully. "But I'm afraid he might get some infection in that wound. He ought to be in hospital, and not fooling about in this filthy swamp."

"We'll get him to one — eventually."

She stared down at him. "How? Where? I can't even see where we can go next."

"We're heading for the coast," he reassured her. "Once there we'll steal a boat and get him to Miami, or some other point off the American mainland. That sounds vague, I know, but that's what we'll do. Now things have got this bad it's the only thing we can do."

She continued to stare, and then slowly she smiled. "Vague must be the understatement of the year. But when you say it, after what you did on that ridge, I'll believe it."

He chuckled and pulled her down beside him.

"Don't have too much faith in me," he said. "On the ridge I was lucky."

She shook her head. "That wasn't luck, I'm sure of it. And I'm sure of something else, you're not just the lecherous salesman you pretended you were back in London."

"But I am," Larren said softly. "And I'll prove it." His hands closed on her shoulders, pressing them to the ground, and then his mouth closed over her lips. She stiffened a moment, and then relaxed, submitting to his lingering embrace.

He could feel the pressure of her breathing beneath him, and felt the answering stirring of her mouth. Her eyes were closed and her body trembled. His hand caressed her shoulder, and then moved in a gradual stroking motion down the length of her body. She stirred uneasily as his palm spread over her hip, and then twisted nervously as his hand touched the hem of her skirt.

She broke her mouth away from his own and said huskily.

"No, Simon, not here. Please."

He smiled. "What's wrong, Caroline. You've never struggled before."

"Simon, this is different. You can't make love in a swamp. Besides, my knees are too sore. I — "

"Caroline, you misjudge me," Larren silenced her sadly. "I'm not intending to make love to you."

She blinked beneath his hard stare, and then abruptly his weight crushed fully against her, pinning her to the ground as his mouth clamped over her own to still her muffled outcry. She squirmed in a helpless fury that was not prompted by any maidenly modesty, but despite her wriggles his hand searched until he found what he had suspected was there. She became still then, and her blue eyes glared at him in angry despair.

Very carefully he traced the outline of the little palm gun, and then he removed it from its position tucked beneath her girdle.

He held the miniature weapon before her eyes and said gently.

"Now that we're on the subject of people who pretend, I must confess that I don't believe that you're an innocent little press photographer any more than I'm an export salesman. So I suggest that we start with you telling the truth to me."

15

Outpost of the Damned

THE little palm gun, as its name implied, was small enough to lie in the palm of Larren's hand. It was barely four inches long, flat, and carried a small calibre bullet for each of the tiny barrels that were set one on top of the other instead of side by side. It looked like a toy, but accurately aimed it could be a very deadly toy. Caroline stared at it as Larren pointed the twin barrels an inch from her nose, and then she looked helplessly into his waiting eyes. She paled a little before their stony gaze, and then said miserably.

"How did you know, Simon?"

"I guessed as we came through the swamp," his voice was clinical and very cold. "While the rest of us were holding our ironmongery above our heads, you were fiddling at the waist of your skirt as though you were also worried about something you didn't want to get wet. You changed your mind pretty quickly when I glanced back, but you were a little too slow." He glanced at the gun and smiled bleakly. "Proper little two-shot Annie, aren't you?"

Her mouth tightened and she refused to answer.

Larren went on softly. "But now let's get back to the explaining bit. And don't tell me that you work for the F.B.I., or the C.I.A., or the Interpol department of the Chinese Treasury. Because I've read all of those in the best spy-cum-fairy stories, and I don't believe that any of them are interested in me." She flinched as he allowed the twin barrels of the miniature pistol to touch her nose, and then he added. "But you could try me with the K.G.B. I could believe that the Russians are interested."

She blinked, and then said simply.

"Don't be bloody ridiculous. I work for Smith."

The quiet answer toppled Larren's self assurance like a sudden wind through a house of cards. His mind groped for a reply, but even though his mind was at a loss his training took control, and as if it were someone else speaking he heard his voice say harshly.

"And who the hell is Smith?"

Quite unexpectedly Caroline smiled.

"Smith is the dear little podgy man who gives both of us our orders. He sits behind a big desk in a Whitehall office, and the last time you were there was eight days ago when he told you that you were to become Jose Rafael's fourth shadow. This San Quito business had prevented him from getting out to lunch that day and so he sent his secretary for sandwiches while you were there. She brought a pot of coffee and a big plate of ham and tomato sandwiches. You made a hog of yourself when he offered and picked out four of the ham ones."

Slowly Larren relaxed, for he had no choice but to believe her now. The secretary had left the office after bringing in the food tray, and only Smith himself had known exactly how many and which kind of those sandwiches Larren had eaten, and the imparting of such irrelevant, but closely factual knowledge was Smith's personal way of identifying one agent to another. He was no longer distrustful, but was still puzzled as he lowered her little gun and demanded.

"But what the devil are you supposed to be doing?"

"Isn't that obvious now? Smith wants a security report on you." Her eyes gleamed with malicious satisfaction as she saw him react, and then she continued. "Smith was worried about your long string of girl friends, the short-time love 'em and leave 'em affairs that seem to make up the whole of your love life. He saw how easily a woman could be planted on to you, and he was worried."

"You mean that Smith considered me a security risk?"

"Now don't get indignant, Simon. Smith simply had to be sure that you could handle this kind of situation if it should ever arise. And so he planted me on to you first. He just wanted to be certain that you were discreet with your girl friends. After all, you have asked for it. You've been through quite a number of different women in the past few years." She chuckled suddenly. "If that isn't too indelicate a way of phrasing it."

Larren was still ruffled, and he ignored the soothing note of humour. He said bluntly.

"But why send you here to San Quito? In fact, if I'm under suspicion, why did he send me?"

She sighed. "Be reasonable, Simon. This suspicion as you call it was merely a routine check, and when this present job appeared you were still the best man available. Smith considers you as a kind of trouble-shooter, and he sensed that this job would become violent. So naturally he sent you. He also wanted someone to report back on the general situation on the island, something you couldn't do while your attention was focused on Rafael, and so he sent me. I'm afraid I didn't do very well though. I was beginning to get some facts that pointed to a connection between the local Communists and the new growth of voodoo, but all that I managed to actually see was a cock-killing ceremony in the jungle, and that didn't help much."

Larren frowned, and said slowly. "But I still don't see why he sent you. The coincidence of you popping up so many times just had to make me suspicious, and that cancels out your value in the security check you were making in London."

She smiled. "That's debatable. By chance I had been given a cover which gave me a legitimate excuse to come here, and Smith reasoned that the awkwardness of having one of your old flames appear in the middle of a job would provide a testing situation for you. I was to continue my original job by reporting on how well you were able to explain yourself." Her smile saddened a little. "You didn't do too well did you — telling me that Reb Hansen was a bicycle millionaire?"

Larren was able to smile in return. "No," he admitted. "I didn't. But what happens now?"

She shrugged. "I report an unfinished mission, with no definite conclusions. And meanwhile I help you to get Dominguez away to safety. That's obviously our combined job now."

He nodded, and then abruptly a memory returned and he asked bluntly. "When you made love to me in London, was that all part of the job?"

She was startled, her blue eyes reflecting anger, and then she seemed to accept that his demand was not unreasonable and answered quietly.

"No, Simon. I honestly enjoyed that. If I hadn't I would never have gone quite so far. It wasn't in my orders."

Larren tried to read her expression, and then slowly he grinned. He kissed her mouth again, and gently replaced her little palm gun exactly where he had found it.

★ ★ ★

Shortly after dawn the next morning they held a brief council of war, and it was immediately clear that their position was worse than Larren had realized. Dominguez, the two army officers and Shaw were the only ones who knew anything of the coastline for which they were headed, and they could only suggest one hope; a penal colony named Blackwater at the mouth of the Black River.

Rafael groaned as though his back had just broken beneath the final straw and said in exasperation.

"A penal colony! What kind of

help can we expect from a horde of convicts?"

"The colony is staffed with prison officers and armed guards," Dominguez explained patiently. "It is they who will help us. Because the colony is isolated by the swamp most of the communication with the rest of the mainland is made by sea by means of two fast government launches. We shall borrow one of those to take us clear of San Quito."

Andy Shaw added emphatically. "I've visited Blackwater on one or two occasions to deliver prisoners, and I know those launches are capable of getting us to the coast of Florida. The colony is only a day's march away, and there's nowhere else where we can hope to find a boat."

Rafael adopted a look of sour resignation and became silent.

Then Larren said pointedly. "What kind of a prison is it — political or hardened criminals?"

The Police Inspector's youthful face

reflected a strained smile. "You've touched the·one dubious point," he admitted. "The settlement houses both kinds — and the political prisoners are mostly trouble-making Communists."

"Which means that they'll be in sympathy with the people now in control, and that there's a chance that Blackwater will have changed hands?"

Shaw nodded. "It's possible, but the rebels will have their hands full in holding Aparicio and rounding up the remnants of Colonel Oparto's army. They can't do everything at once, and releasing political prisoners will probably take second place. We'll have to approach warily until we're sure, but as I said before, there's no other place where we can get a boat."

Larren nodded in reluctant agreement, and then Dominguez said with finality.

"Inspector Shaw has presented the facts very clearly, and I think that ends any need for any further discussion. The sooner we get moving and reach Blackwater, the greater are the chances of finding normal conditions and obtaining a boat." He struggled to his feet and the two army officers moved swiftly to help him. The rest of them, who had squatted in a half circle around him, rose to follow his example. Dominguez glanced at Zamora and said.

"Thank you, Major. Now tell the escort detail that we are ready to go. By heading a little north of east we should strike into the Black River close to the penal settlement sometime in the late afternoon."

* * *

That day was one of the foulest that Larren could ever remember. He was no stranger to grim conditions, but the evil, stagnant waters of the swamp surpassed anything he had yet encountered. The lower half of his body was almost continuously immersed, while the upper half dripped sweat in the cloying heat. Overhanging branches whipped at his face and he tripped and stumbled endlessly over the underwater roots of the mangroves. The soldiers who led the way were in an even more luckless position, for from time to time they floundered wholly out of their depth as they endeavoured to find a passable route.

Dominguez's face was grey with pain, as he struggled gamely between Shaw and Zamora, and Larren was now helping the uncomplaining Caroline Brand. Larren was worried about both the President and the girl, for he was well aware of what the filth of the swamp could do to their wounds.

Behind them Sam Friday was assisting Rafael, while Reb Hansen seemed to be dividing his time equally between the wounded Sanchez and Rosemary Keene. Both the Mexican and the redhead were maintaining an almost complete silence. Sanchez tight-lipped against the pain of his arm, and Rosemary seemingly listless and defeated. Delgado was again bringing up the rear with two soldiers, all of them with sten guns ready to blast any inquisitive crocodile.

Caroline began to stumble more and more frequently as the day progressed, each time wincing with pain. Finally she would have sprawled headlong and gone under if it had not been for Larren's support, and her face twisted with the first signs of tears as she clung against him. She said nothing, but just leaned her head against his panting chest as the black water slapped around her thighs. Larren's unsmiling mouth grew even tighter, and equally silently he lifted her up. Then carrying her in his arms he pushed on determinedly.

He held her legs above water, and saw that the bandages round her torn knees were now trailing in useless, sopping strips of rag. But there was nothing he could do. After a while she told him to set her down but he ignored her, wading methodically in Dominguez's wake. Her weight began to tear at his arms and shoulders, and his spine began to feel like a drawn bow that must eventually splinter and break. The sweat rolled down his face in steady streams.

And then a big hand closed on his shoulder.

"Put her down, man." Sam Friday was breathing heavily, but he still looked colossally fit. "You go back and take care of the boss. I'll look after your little lady."

Larren hesitated, and then allowed Caroline to stand upright. The big negro grinned at them and then knelt low.

"Climb on my back," he ordered. "Old Sam's big enough to carry the two of us."

Caroline obeyed awkwardly, straddling his shoulders. And then Friday lifted her up. The extra weight seemed to have no effect on the brawny negro, and with another amiable grin at Larren he strode off to catch up with the two men helping Dominguez.

Larren waited for Rafael to catch him

up, and saw the look of anger in the man's savage eyes. It was clear that Maraquilla's President resented the way his bodyguards were beginning to act without waiting for his express orders, but he either saw the futility or was too tired to argue. Larren decided that Rafael could help himself and simply walked beside him.

The sun, barely penetrating their damp, shadowed world, passed slowly overhead, Larren found it impossible to judge how far they had travelled and could only measure their progress in hours. Sometimes the ground rose and allowed them to walk on soggy grass where they could make better time, but for the most part the weight of the water pushing against their legs made their advance slow. Leeches fastened on to their skin, and once Rosemary Keene screamed as a six foot snake swam slowly along the surface of the water.

They rested for an hour at noon, opening a few tins of meat from the soldiers packs, and drinking sparingly from the fast emptying water bottles. Then again they plunged on through the swamp.

For another three hours they slithered, splashed and stumbled through their ghastly world, and then abruptly the ground began to rise until they were once more clear of the hampering waters. The foliage became thick before them, and the weary soldiers again drew their bayonets to hack a passage through the virgin barrier. Five minutes later they found themselves on the bank of a fast swirling river. They stopped, blinking in the sudden glare of the sun, and then Andy Shaw announced between gulps for air that they had reached the Black River, and that the penal settlement could not be more than a mile below them.

Rosemary Keene had already sprawled thankfully on the grass, and Sam Friday carefully lowered Caroline Brand beside her. The rest of them stared at the treacherous surface of the river, it was black with swamp mud and very fitting to its name. They laboured for breath for a moment, and then Larren said.

"Now all we've got to do is check that we're not walking into more trouble, and that seems like my kind of job again."

Shaw said weakly. "I'll go with you."

Larren looked at him, and saw that he was near to exhaustion from the efforts of helping Zamora with Dominguez, and shook his head.

"You'd best stay with the President," he said tactfully. Then he glanced at Reb Hansen and added. "But I might need a bit of help — a veteran from Guadalcanal would be ideal."

Hansen grinned. "My pleasure, Larren. Let's get on with it."

★ ★ ★

They borrowed two bayonets from the escort detail, and it took them almost an hour to hack their way along the river bank and come within sight of the penal settlement. Where it was possible they waded in the shallows of the river, but for the most part the ugly waters were too swift and deep. They were again sweating and breathing hard when Hansen finally touched Larren's arm and indicated the top of a wooden watchtower that just showed around the bend of the river.

He said grimly. "I guess that's it."

Larren nodded, and checked the Smith & Wesson, which he had hung around his neck to keep it clear of the swamp. The gun felt cold and damp but he hoped that it was still serviceable. Hansen fished his own Colt from his armpit holster and they moved slowly forward.

As they turned the bend they were able to see the full layout of the Blackwater settlement. It was a town of wooden buildings built entirely on a large sandbank island in the mouth of the river. It was totally surrounded by a fifteen foot palisade of pointed poles, and the whole was dominated by two of the tall watchtowers, placed just inside the palisade at either end. The land on either side of the settlement had been cleared completely of jungle, and the flat fields had been clearly cultivated by working parties of prisoners. However, there were no convicts in view now, and the whole settlement seemed strangely silent. The machine guns in the watch towers were unmanned, and that, to Larren, spelt the worst.

"What do you think?" he asked softly.

"It gives me that feeling," Hansen answered. "The one that crawls up your back when you stop to wonder where the next Jap is coming from."

"Me too, only in my case they were Germans."

"Hmmmm, let's get a little closer." Hansen rose from his crouching position and began to pad silently forward.

Larren followed, and then quietly reached out to touch the American's arm. Hansen looked back, and then followed the direction of Larren's pointing finger.

On the far side of the river what at first appeared to be a black log was snagged in the reeds, rolling slightly from side to side with the movement of the current. It took a second, closer scrutiny to recognize it as a body in a black uniform.

Larren said grimly. "Only the guards would wear uniform."

Hansen nodded. "I guess that settles it," he said slowly. "We're out of luck. That place looks like an outpost of the damned, and if they've chopped down the guards then the damned have taken over."

16

Betrayed

LARREN and Hansen crouched low in the reeds, ignoring the half-submerged corpse jammed against the far bank and again concentrating on the grim stockade of the Blackwater penal settlement. The uncanny silence still persisted, except for the shrill cries of the river birds and the swish and gurgle of the current through the shoals. The sun was hot on their backs and drawing wisps of steam from their damp clothes. They were still almost three hundred yards away from the point where the river split into two forks around the island enclosure, and were not quite close enough to decide whether or not it was deserted. Finally they exchanged speculative glances, and then by mutual consent began to close the gap, hunching low to use the cover along the river bank.

They advanced another fifty yards, and in that distance counted three more dead bodies trapped in the shallows. All of them wore the black uniform of Government prison guards. Larren began to feel a looseness in his bowels, and he wondered how many more corpses had been carried into the swamp to bloat the ever-hungry bellies of the crocodiles.

For the next hundred yards they crawled, and finally they slithered the last stretch on their stomachs. They could see a thin curl of smoke now, rising towards the far watchtower from a dying fire. That, and the faint sound of movement, told them that the settlement was still occupied.

Hansen turned his head as he lay on his chest in the reeds, and murmured softly.

"I guess a bunch of the rebels arrived during the night or early this morning. But they'd only want the political prisoners. The rest of the cons must be free but still there."

Larren nodded slowly in agreement. "They must have taken the colony by surprise, and no doubt the convicts grabbed their chance to attack the guards from behind. The prison staff must have been slaughtered wholesale." He paused to study the stockade and then continued. "Right now I guess they're taking it easy from the heat, and they won't be expecting any interruption. So now that we've got this far I think we ought to circle round to the river mouth and see if there is any transport left. It's unlikely, I know, but it's not impossible."

"Seems like we're clutching at straws." Hansen smiled wryly, and then he wriggled forward to lead the way.

There was little chance of their being detected from behind the fifteen foot palisade that was now directly opposite them across the river, but if anyone had chanced to mount one of the two watchtowers any open movement would have been seen immediately, and so they played safe. Occasionally they heard the mutter of voices above the splash and ripple of the river, but the sounds were muffled and Larren became convinced that the convicts must be enjoying a late siesta from the sluggish afternoon heat. Probably they had celebrated after their release, and if there had been any liquor in the Governor's stores they were most likely drunk.

Ahead of them they saw a bridge, a roughly constructed affair of wooden logs that connected the far end of the island with the mainland. It was built where it could be overlooked by the second watchtower, and Larren guessed that there would be a similar bridge on the other side of the settlement to give access to the fields on the far bank of the river.

They approached the bridge with care, and saw that the heavy wooden gates that gave entry to the stockade on the far side were wide open. They could see vague movements inside that showed that even though they were quiet not all of the convicts were asleep.

They advanced another few yards, and then stopped when they had obtained a broken view of the mouth of the river beyond the island where it widened to meet the Caribbean sea. They were close to the bridge now, shielded by a clump of bush and vegetation, and the risks would be doubled if they attempted to pass in front of the bridge and the open gates beyond. However, those risks were not necessary, for they could see all that they needed from here. The sight was unexpected, and made them both stiffen with surprise. For there, lying silently at anchor in the deepening water, were two sleek grey gunboats.

Larren stared at the two high-bowed craft lying side by side, seeing the sunlight flash and glitter on their steel plates and the polished barrels of the black muzzled guns. There were soldiers patrolling their decks, quietly, lazily, but heavily armed. They looked two very efficient fighting ships.

Hansen whistled very softly through his teeth. "It looks as though the rebel mob are still here," he said. "I wonder why?"

Larren frowned dubiously. "Perhaps they stopped to celebrate their victory with the prisoners. Or perhaps they just don't know how to pull out without another battle. They can't take all the convicts with them, and the ones who have to be left behind obviously wouldn't like it."

"Maybe," Hansen sounded even more dubious. Then his tone sharpened. "See there, they must be the two launches that Shaw talked about."

Larren stopped his thoughtful appraisal of the two gun-boats and followed the American's pointing finger to the left. He saw a long wooden jetty built on to the far bank. Two armed sentries from the gunboats were marching slowly up and down its narrow length, and tied against it were two large launches.

Larren stopped wondering why the rebel forces were still here, and his mouth began to form a smile. "Only two guards," he commented. "That's careless to say the least. You and I could take them without difficulty. After dark of course. We can sabotage the launch we don't want, and with luck we can get away along the coast before the gun-boats can pull anchor."

Hansen grimaced. "And if we're not lucky the gunboats will blast us all into the wild blue yonder. But — " He shrugged. "It's a chance. And I can't see any other."

"Let's get back," Larren said. "We'll see whether Dominguez or Shaw can suggest any alternatives."

Hansen nodded, and equally carefully they began to wriggle back the way they had come.

It took them almost thirty minutes to get back up the river to the edge of the jungle behind the cultivated fields.

They were able to stand fully upright then, and gratefully straightened their aching backs. Hansen slipped his gun back beneath his armpit, and Larren returned the Smith & Wesson to the spring-loaded holster that now dangled from around his neck. They rested up for a few moments, and then again drew their borrowed bayonets and began to cut their way back to where they had left their companions.

As he worked Larren's mind was fully occupied with the flimsy threads of his plan to commandeer one of the two launches. He knew that provided the guard was not strengthened at night then he and Hansen could easily account for the two sentries on the jetty, but he was more worried by the threat of the gunboats than he cared to admit. Whichever way he looked at it the scheme was a gamble, and yet he had to get Dominguez and the other wounded members of the party out of the swamp, otherwise those wounds would become poisonous or gangrenous. The fact that they were almost out of food and water was another calculation that could not be ignored.

They made the return journey more slowly, for they were both tired, and they knew that any kind of action would be impossible before nightfall anyway. They rested several times, squatting breathlessly in the tangles of fern and branches that clogged the river bank. Conversation was a waste of effort, and so they were mostly silent but for the panting of their exertions. The chop and click of the bayonets became a rhythm of dull music that merged with the rushing of the Black River.

Once they stopped, waiting motionless as a nine-foot crocodile slithered slowly out of their way. It was the only one they saw at close quarters but they knew that the swamp was infested with the brutes. Hansen commented that they were too well fed on prison guards to be looking for fresh meat, and then the two men continued on their way.

The sun was lowering now, and the shadows were growing stronger, and they began to hurry a little as they realized that they had delayed too long. They still had another quarter mile to go to reach their companions, and then abruptly they heard the muffled sounds of gunfire up ahead.

They stopped, breaking the rhythm of chopping bayonets as they listened tensely. The gunfire continued in coughing bursts of sound, violating the silence with the ferocity of a full scale battle.

"Goddamn!" Hansen said savagely, and then the bayonet whirled in his hand as he began to run.

Larren sprinted at his heels, splashing through the shallows of the river as they rushed towards the sounds of conflict.

★ ★ ★

The shooting was over long before they reached the scene, and the matted barrier of fern and branches had

301

checked their headlong advance. They still hurried as much as possible, but a multitude of cuts from the springing vegetation had forced them to approach more sanely and use their bayonets with proper effect. The bayonets were not quite heavy enough for the job now expected of them, and their wrists were aching from the extra effort needed to slice through the thicker branches. They were both streaming sweat again, and were thankful when they were near enough for caution to become more important than speed.

The bayonets were thrust into their belts, and both men drew their guns as they covered the last hundred yards. They moved the restraining foliage gently with their left hands, and trod carefully to avoid any undue noise, Larren's chest was echoing the thumping of his heart, and his palms were again moist. There was no sound ahead of them now, and when they reached the spot where they had left Dominguez and the others they saw

302

two of their soldier escort sprawled lifeless in the grass.

They stopped, listening, and with every other sense alert. There was no sound but for those of the river, but the dank atmosphere was mingled with traces of smoke and cordite. There was the quietness of death, and the faint, sticky scent of blood.

Warily Larren moved from cover to inspect the two dead soldiers. Hansen stayed back, watching for any reaction from the silent jungle. Nothing happened, and slowly the American came into the open.

The first two soldiers had both been shot through the chest, and as they searched further they found the sergeant and five more of the twelve man escort detail lying dead. The lifeless body of Major Zamora stared up at them from a patch of fern, and Larren heard Hansen curse in a bitter undertone as he came upon the equally still figure of Sanchez Lorenzo. A bullet had smashed into the Mexican's temple, and he lay on his stomach with his good hand trapped beneath him where he had been reaching for his automatic.

Hansen looked up and said tightly. "Someone's got to pay for this. Sanchez has been my buddy for a long time."

At the sound of his raised voice there was a sudden movement from the tangle of undergrowth behind them, and both men wheeled as though triggered by the same spring. The Smith & Wesson and the sawn-off Colt were both cocked towards the sound, and then the rustle came again.

"Reb! Reb, don't shoot — it's me."

They both recognized the frightened voice as Rosemary Keene struggled towards them. She was pale and bedraggled and her flowing mane of fiery hair was littered with black leaves and pieces of twig. Hansen plunged forward to meet her and she tumbled into his arms.

"Rose, honey, take it easy." The American cradled her against his chest as she sobbed helplessly. "Rose, for

Christ's sake! Tell us what happened?"

Larren lowered his gun and went to join them. He gripped the girl's shoulder hard and said levelly.

"You've only got to tell us once, Rosemary. You can cry later."

She looked at him, and then her gaze turned back to Hansen's face. Her head dropped to his shoulder again and she said falteringly.

"It — it was horrible. They didn't have a chance. Those people just appeared and started shooting." She swallowed hard and then said. "Shaw — Shaw is still alive. He's back there."

Hansen looked at Larren, but Larren was already thrusting past them. He followed the passage that the girl had made, and after a few yards found Andy Shaw lying against the slime-black trunk of a rotting tree. The young Police Inspector was unconscious, and there was blood on his face from a nasty bullet crease across the temple. Larren crouched beside him and saw that he was otherwise unharmed.

Larren jammed his gun into his waistband, and for a moment he struggled to lift Shaw alone. Then Hansen appeared behind him and together they carried the policeman's limp weight out into the open where Rosemary was still trembling a little. She came to help as they laid Shaw down, and then said weakly.

"He was the first to be hit. I was sitting close by him and I dragged him with me into the bushes. The others were all caught in the open and the soldiers just went spinning down like pins in a bowling alley." She was in control of herself now and went on. "They wanted Dominguez and Rafael alive. They took Sam and Caroline Brand too. I think Sam was hurt."

"What about the rest of the soldiers?" Larren asked. "There's four of them unaccounted for."

"They — they just herded them to one side, and then shot them down. It was after they were taken prisoners.

The bodies are a little further back in the jungle."

"Delgado too?"

"No!" Her voice became sharp and wretchedly bitter. "It was Lieutenant Delgado who led them here. I noticed that he'd slipped away about an hour before it happened, but I didn't give it any thought. Then when the shooting started I saw that he was with them. He was the one who shot Sanchez."

Hansen's face hardened into savagery, but Larren was puzzled.

"Rosemary, who were these people?"

"Rebels of course. They came from Blackwater. There were even a few convicts with them."

"But it's taken us the best part of three and a half hours to get to Blackwater and back. How did Delgado manage it in an hour?"

"It was easy. There's a proper path on the other side of the river. I don't know how Delgado knew about it when Shaw didn't, but I heard him gloating to Dominguez." She drew a deep breath and then finished. "I don't know whether Delgado was a traitor all along, or whether he just made up his mind to switch on to the winning side. In any case it hardly matters now."

She became silent, and after a moment Hansen asked.

"What happens now, Larren?"

Larren's unsmiling face was expressionless. He said flatly.

"First we'll revive Shaw, just in case they come back. Delgado knows that you and I are still loose, and he might be a perfectionist."

"I almost hope he is." Hansen said bleakly. "I'd just love to have him come looking for me."

Larren said nothing, but started on the task of bringing the young policeman back to consciousness. Rosemary offered a handkerchief that had been tucked in the belt of her dress and he used it to clean the blood from Shaw's face. Shaw stirred and his mouth twisted against the return of pain.

Five minutes later the young Inspector

was sitting up, and complaining of a splitting headache. He looked groggy, but was already showing a tough capacity for recovery. When Larren told him what had happened he muttered a typically British, "Damn and Blast," and then asked the same question as Hansen had done.

"What happens now?"

Larren knelt on one knee facing him, and his eyes were very determined. He said grimly.

"Reb and I spotted those two launches you told us about, and we reckon that we're capable of taking one once it gets dark. They're not too heavily guarded." He paused, trying to read the reaction in the other man's eyes, then went on. "But first I'm going to have a shot at pulling Dominguez and the others out of that penal colony. Dominguez because he's vital to any hope of restoring peace to San Quito, and Rafael because technically he's still my responsibility. I'm hoping that you can draw me the layout of the place, and tell me where I can best expect to find them."

Shaw said slowly. "The most likely place will be the solitary cells, because they are the most solid and they'll be empty. But you won't need a diagram, because I'm coming with you."

Larren smiled. "I half expected you to say that, and I'll be glad to have you." He turned his head then to look up at Reb Hansen. The American was holding one arm close around Rosemary Keene, while his free hand still held the short-nosed Colt. Larren didn't need to ask, for Hansen was already speaking in a cold, lazy drawl.

"That sounds like fun, Larren, so I guess I'll string along. I haven't had any real, genuine fun since Guadalcanal."

17

A Traitor Unmasked

AN hour after nightfall Simon Larren crouched at the jungle's edge only fifty yards from the long jetty that moored the two government launches belonging to the penal settlement. Out in the river mouth the two rebel gunboats still lay at anchor, their silhouettes black and forbidding in the cloud-broken starlight. The night was filled with creaks and rustlings from the invisible world of the jungle, and with the croaking sing-song of a colony of frogs along the marshy bank of the river. The only other sounds were the even tread of the two sentries marching slowly up and down the jetty, and the low, laboured breathing of Rosemary Keene who crouched at Larren's side.

Down the river, beyond the jetty, the outline of the two watchtowers and the spiked palisade of Blackwater's enclosure were faintly visible. And somewhere down there, hidden by darkness, were Reb Hansen and Andy Shaw. By now the two men should be concealed close to the bridge, for although they were now on the north side of the river Larren had been right in guessing that there would be an identical bridge to the one he and Hansen had approached earlier along the south bank. For the next half hour the two men would keep watch through the open gates of the stockade, noting the movements of the men inside, and assessing the chances of liberating Dominguez and his fellow captives. In the meantime Larren had undertaken to ensure their escape route and leave Rosemary aboard one of the launches in readiness for a quick getaway before he joined the rescue attempt.

The night was warm, but Larren

felt Rosemary shivering a little as she pressed against him. Their clothing was still wet from the brief dip when they had been forced to swim across the lower reaches of the river to find the cleared path that had been used by the traitorous Lieutenant Delgado, and there was no sun now to dry them out. Larren placed his hand on her arm and said softly.

"Are you okay?"

He sensed the brief nod of her head in the darkness, and then she said. "I'm just a little bit cold, that's all."

"Then this is where we part company," he said quietly. "All you have to do is to sit tight and wait until I call you. And don't panic if I seem to be gone for too long, because this sort of job can't be hurried. I have to pick the right moment."

She nodded a second time, her hair brushing his shoulder. "Don't worry about me. I won't enjoy sitting on the edge of a swampy jungle full of creepy crawlies, but I can stick it till you get back."

Larren gave her arm a parting squeeze, and then he left her alone, merging like an unseen ghost into the blackness. The grass rustled slightly beneath his feet, but not enough for the sound to be distinguishable from all the other movements of the night. He still had the bayonet in his belt, but he preferred his own blade for the task ahead, and drew it carefully from inside his jacket. His gun he had left with Rosemary, for bullets would be too noisy.

He moved out into the river, feeling the mud suck at his feet and the water lap around his ankles as he stepped through the reeds. The hoarse croaking of the frogs became more agitated, and something splashed further along the bank. Larren hesitated, but then kept going. The black water crept to his knees and then to his thighs. It washed around his waist, and then he took the knife in his teeth and slowly and silently he began to swim.

The tide was rising, and he allowed its movement to float him down to the furthest launch which was tied to the end of the jetty. Only his head broke the surface, and his movements were just enough to keep him from going underwater. The current carried him underneath the bows of the launch and then he bumped gently against one of the poles that supported the jetty.

He stayed there for a few moments, steadying his heartbeat, and breathing carefully through his nose. Then he slowly pulled himself from one support to the next, listening closely as he passed the length of the launch. There was no sound from the motionless craft, and no suggestion of life through the black holes of the open ports. Larren drew a deep breath and slowly swam towards shore and the second launch, using the poles to draw himself along beneath the jetty. The second craft was also silent and empty, and after he had made certain that this was so he permitted himself a faint smile. All he had to deal with were the two sentries on the jetty itself.

From time to time the sentries had taken it in turn to walk up and down the length of the jetty, but at the moment they were talking quietly towards the landward end. Larren swam slowly towards them through the blackness, with the rough boards less than two feet above his head. The faintest of ripples marked his progress, but the noise was lost amongst the slight lapping of the water around the supports.

When he was directly beneath the two men he found that he was able to stand up. The inky water lapped around his chest, and there was a gap of a bare few inches above his head. He removed the knife from his teeth and waited.

It was ten minutes before the sentries separated to make their routine check, and at last Larren heard the hollow tread of footsteps as one of them walked towards the far end, presumably to check on the two launches. The second man remained where he was.

Larren filled his chest with air, and then ducked silently beneath the surface. He had to make two strong, downward strokes before his hands felt the mud on the bottom, and he groped swiftly to find a stone. His fingers curled around one and he allowed his body to float up and right itself. He paused a moment to adjust his balance and ease his chest, and then he moved carefully to one side. He waited by the outer poles of the jetty, and then skimmed the stone between the surface of the water and the boards so that it splashed on the far side.

The knife was between his teeth again as he heard the sentry start, and then move away from him to investigate the splash. Swiftly Larren's hands gripped the edge of the jetty just above his head, and with one easy movement he drew himself up from the water and balanced on his hands. The sentry was three yards away, with his back turned as he bent forward to peer into the river. Larren swung his feet up on to the jetty, thrust upright, and snatched the knife from his teeth as he leaped forward. The sentry had heard the slight creak of the planks and started to turn. He was half way round as Larren crashed into him. Larren's arm curled around the man's neck as his hand clamped over the opening mouth, and the knife flashed once as they toppled over the jetty and back into the river.

Larren hung on to the dead sentry as they went under, and then found his feet again and pulled the body into the blackness between the supports.

The second sentry was already calling softly to his companion, and Larren heard his steps approaching along the boards. The man had heard the moment of splashing, but he had been too far away to see anything and was simply asking what had happened. Larren remained silent, and as he expected the sentry's steps became more wary.

Larren raised his palm, and slapped on the surface of the water. The sentry stopped at the sound and then came near to the edge. Larren could see nothing of him but the downward pointing snout of a sten gun as he searched the gloom.

Carefully Larren gave the body he was holding a firm push, sending it out into the open where the tide immediately started to turn it back a few feet nearer the shore.

The man on the jetty gave a gasp, and then crouched low for a closer look at the drifting corpse. And then Larren reached up to grab his wrist close to the sten gun and pull him sharply forward. There was a second splash as the man hit the water, and then Larren was dragged sideways by his struggles. For a moment they grappled, and then the expertly-lunged knife scored its second kill. Larren released the body, panting slightly, and hauled himself up on to the jetty. He stood for a moment, and then returned the knife to his dripping jacket and called softly to Rosemary Keene.

A minute passed, and he called again, and then he heard her approaching from the river bank. She flinched when he found her and his hand touched her arm, and she asked hoarsely.

"The sentries, what — what happened?"

He chuckled. "They're at the Golden Gates, asking St. Peter the very same question."

He sensed her shiver, and then he took her arm and led her along the jetty. He made her wait again while he boarded the first launch and made a quick inspection, and before he left he wrecked enough of the engine to ensure that it could not be used for any possible pursuits later during the night. Then he rejoined the redhead and escorted her to the second launch.

He helped her to climb aboard, and allowed her to precede him into the roomy cabin. He moved around the bulkheads and carefully closed all the ports, and then screwed shut the steel port covers. The cabin was in inky blackness when he had finished, and no light could penetrate in or out. He felt safe then in switching on the electric light.

Rosemary blinked in the sudden glare, and then looked slowly around her. After a moment she looked at him and gave a forced smile.

"I'll be okay now, Larren. I know what to do — get the launch started if there's any racket behind you when you come back, and just stay quiet until you get here if there isn't."

Larren nodded. "That's right, but before I go I'll need my gun."

"Of course," she fumbled at the belt of her dress and pulled out his Smith & Wesson. She handed it over, and then slowly her smile faded as she looked into his face. For instead of returning the gun to its holster, which was now belted around his waist again, he was pointing it sadly at her stomach.

She swallowed hard. "What — What are you doing?"

Larren said quietly. "It's very simple, Rosemary. The situation has now reached the point where I have to be sure of everyone behind me before I go sticking my neck out. And that means that before I leave you in charge of our only escape route I have to be doubly sure of you."

She stared. "What are you talking about?"

He explained patiently. "I'm talking about the main reason why I was sent to act as Rafael's fourth shadow. It was because Rafael couldn't fully trust the three shadows he'd already got. There had been two attempts on his life and he was certain that someone who had to be really close to him was involved."

He paused, and then said bluntly. "One of those attempts was by using poison, and I've been wondering who out of all the possibles would be the most likely to choose that method. It wouldn't be Sanchez, he would have used a knife. And it wouldn't be Sam either. Sam would have used a gun, or his hands perhaps, something basic and simple. Then there's Reb. He might have used a knife, a gun, his hands, or a dozen other tricks they taught him in the Marines — but never poison. Those three are all killers, but they're violent killers. I don't think poison as a means of murder would even occur to any of them. That only seems to leave you, doesn't it, Rosemary? And that fits the facts, because most poisoners are usually women."

"That's crazy." The redhead was tight-lipped and angry. "Why should I want to kill Jose?"

Larren smiled. "I can think of a dozen reasons. A dictator is the kind of man who asks to be killed. And an arrogant dictator like Rafael asks louder than most."

"But why pick on me?" She was both angry and scared.

"Because, as I've already said, it has

to be someone who was very close — and I mean *very* close. I've noticed the way that Sam always slips off to check the kitchens before any meals are served, and it's a sure bet that he wouldn't forget to sample the wines. That means that the poison that was introduced to Rafael's glass before he left Maraquilla must have been added practically at the table. And who but his mistress would be sitting beside him at the table?"

She said flatly. "I still say you're crazy. And I don't see how you can prove otherwise."

"It is a problem," Larren admitted. "But it's not unsolvable. If I am right — and I'm almost certain that I am — then there's a strong possibility that you're still carrying some of the stuff with you. A small pill or a capsule could be concealed practically anywhere, and as you nearly succeeded the last time it's reasonable to suppose that you might he prepared for an opportunity to crop up again. And

I have noticed one or two signs of clumsiness or hesitation when you've been eating beside Rafael at some of the receptions we've attended, as though the thought of it disturbs your mind when the opportunities begin to seem possible."

As he talked he had watched her face, and as the tight-lipped expression of anger gave way more and more before the signs of fear, he knew that he was right. He had to finish what he had started now and said evenly.

"Are you going to tell me the truth, Rosemary? Or do I have to find out for myself by searching you inch by inch?"

Her face paled, and she said desperately. "There's nothing to find."

Larren shrugged. "All right, so you won't spare your own blushes. The only alternative is to start taking off your clothes and hand them to me one at a time."

She swallowed hard, and then blurted harshly. "Reb Hansen will kill you for this!"

"Why should Reb do that? I thought you were Rafael's mistress?"

She glared at him, and then angrily she unbelted her dress. She reached to her shoulder blades and practically tore at the supporting zip. She struggled out of the garment and kicked it towards him.

Larren picked it up, and then rested his gun in his holster. He kept his eyes on her face as he ran the wet dress slowly between his hands, feeling with his fingers for any slight bulge that might be sewn into the seams. Finally he dropped it again.

"Let's try the shoes," he suggested.

She kicked them off and he examined them one at a time. There were no false heels or cavities and again he shrugged.

"All right, and the rest."

She said bitterly. "You might at least turn your back."

He smiled. "That's one thing I never do. But if it makes you feel any better you can turn yours."

She said nothing, but her mouth compressed tightly as she unhooked her bra and held it towards him. She stood there proudly as he examined it and made no attempt to turn round. When he returned it she let it fall with her dress. She stepped out of her last garment as though she hoped to gain some element of satisfaction by seeing him embarrassed, but Larren looked over the flimsy scrap of black lace with the same detached scrutiny that he had applied to the rest of her clothing.

She said sourly. "Are you satisfied?"

Larren glanced slowly over her naked body, and realized again how beautiful and wholly female she really was. There was a pride in her nakedness that gave her even more stature than when clothed, as though she knew what the sight of her was doing to him, and felt that the situation was under her control. And then he looked into her eyes and a flicker of doubt appeared as he pointed the Smith & Wesson at her navel.

He said softly. "When I said I'd search you inch by inch, I meant exactly that."

A new fury flared in her eyes, but with it a new fear. She flinched as he touched her, but after a moment he found what he was seeking. The strip of tape was underneath the soft, falling curve of her left breast, and she winced sharply as he pulled it away. The little tape was just over an inch long, and a small, translucent capsule still adhered to the sticky side.

Larren said calmly. "So I was right — and this is it."

Rosemary said nothing, and then abruptly the silence between them was broken as a heavy boot kicked open the cabin door behind Larren's back. The redhead stiffled a cry of alarm, pressing back against the bulkhead. Her eyes had widened with a new, sharper thrust of fear, but almost immediately her expression relaxed into relief.

Larren smiled at her, and then said quietly.

"Come in, Reb, and close the door. We don't want anyone to see the light."

He heard the creak of the single step that led down into the cabin, and then the sound of the door closing. Only then did he return the Smith & Wesson to its holster, raise his hands carefully, and turn to face the ugly nose of Hansen's sawn-off Colt. He said calmly.

"You took longer than I expected, Reb."

Hansen's face was savage. He said tersely.

"So you expected me, huh? You're too damned smart for your own good, Larren. I hope you got a smart explanation to stop me putting a slug in your guts."

Larren held out his hand, showing the poison capsule that rested in his palm. "This is my explanation. I was pretty sure that Rosemary was trying to kill Rafael, and I didn't want any more Delgado-type stabs in the back."

He paused, and then went on evenly. "I was pretty sure that you were with her, Reb. It began to show in the swamp when the going was rough. I figured that if I was right, then you would eventually tumble to why I sent you with Shaw, and brought Rosemary with me."

Hansen said coldly. "You figured right. Shaw's a tough kid, despite that crack on the head. He doesn't need a nursemaid. I began to wonder why you didn't want my help with those two sentries when that should have been a two-man job. I knew you were capable all right, but it began to seem that you were taking an unnecessary risk by going it alone. And I didn't rate you as the type to play hero for the sake of it. That's when I decided it was time I drifted over here to take a look." He smiled bleakly, and then looked at Rosemary. "Are you okay, honey?"

The redhead nodded. "I've had rougher times with Rafael," she said wryly.

Hansen returned his gaze to Larren, but his grey eyes were still frigid.

Larren said. "I take it that you're both employed by Savalas?"

Hansen's mouth curled sharply. "Hell, no. That two-bit sonofabitch would be no better than Rafael. He'd set up another one-man, Hitler state rule and we'd be right back where we started." He grinned lazily. "There are other contenders for Maraquilla, Larren, contenders who'd give a half-starved, trampled population a chance to live."

Larren said. "So now I know where you stand. Now I'll outline my position. My orders were to protect Rafael while he's a guest on San Quito — what happens after that I couldn't care less. So unless you intend to use that gun and cut me down where I stand, I still intend to go ahead with our original plans. I've no doubt you left Shaw watching the settlement, and I know I can count on his help."

He paused, and then finished seriously.

"But Shaw's only a copper. He's willing but he hasn't got the right kind of experience. And in any case, it's more than a two-man job. To stand a fair chance of success I still need a veteran from Guadalcanal."

Hansen stared at him, and then slowly the American began to chuckle. "Goddamn you, Larren. I could hate your guts, but I like your gall." He lowered the Colt and finished. "Sometime I'm going to flatten your jaw for stripping my woman, but right now I guess we've got a job to do."

18

Night of Fury

ANDY SHAW twisted nervously as Larren and Hansen wriggled down beside him in the darkness, but almost immediately he relaxed again.

"You had me worried," he said in a low voice. "I was beginning to think it was time that I came to look for the pair of you."

Hansen smiled. "Larren had everything under control," he murmured blandly. "I just worried too soon."

Larren inched forward through the bed of fern that concealed them close to the bridge, hoping fervently that there were no snakes coiled in the mouldy blackness below his face. He studied the fire-lit enclosure through the open gates on the opposite side of the river, and grimaced as he saw the lone sentry that barred their way. He asked softly.

"What's the score, Andy? Do you think we can pull it off?"

"It's not impossible." Larren could almost picture Shaw's frown as the young Inspector spoke. "There was a bit of noise and movement when Reb and I first arrived, but it's all quietened down now, and I think they've settled for the night. There's only that one sentry, and so far nobody has come out to check that he's at his post. Discipline seems slack and it doesn't look as though they're expecting any trouble."

Hansen grunted. "I wouldn't bet on that. Delgado may believe that you're dead, but the skunk knows damn well that Larren and I are about somewhere."

"I don't think that worries him," Larren murmured. "As far as he is concerned we're just paid bodyguards, and he's probably convinced himself that we're too busy saving our own skins to give him much bother." He paused. "I'm going in."

Hansen smiled in the darkness. "Then I'll take the lead. So far you've claimed all the fun, and I'm kinda curious to see whether I'm still as good as I used to be."

Larren hesitated, but then gave way. Hansen snaked past him and vanished from sight and hearing into the night. Shaw wormed up against Larren's side and they both watched the unsuspecting sentry on the far side of the bridge.

For five minutes they waited, hearing nothing but the routine noises of jungle and river, and then Shaw stiffened slightly with anticipation. Larren strained his eyes and saw a dark shadow emerging from the river close to the far side of the bridge. The swift pounce as the shadow leapt at the sentry was both cat-like and efficient, and as the shadow and victim withdrew swiftly into the blackness below the bridge Larren knew that Reb Hansen had forgotten nothing that the Marines had taught him.

Silently Larren and Shaw rose to their feet and hurried forward. There was no need now to swim the river as Hansen had done, and they crouched low as they moved swiftly across the bridge. Hansen rose to meet them on the far side, his clothes still dripping water, and a moment later all three were pressed against the palisade beside the open gateway.

Hansen had taken a sten gun from the man he had just killed, and now he offered his short Colt to Shaw. The policeman accepted it grimly, and then edged forward to glance through the gateway. He surveyed the interior for perhaps three seconds, and then signalled them to follow as he slipped inside.

Immediately to their right was a square guardhouse built of rough stone. Normally it would have housed the duty officers manning the gate to check the working parties being taken to and from the fields, but now it was empty and Shaw quickly wrenched open the door and dodged inside. Larren was close at his heels and Hansen was only a second behind. All three crouched low behind the heavy desk, which with a large filing cabinet formed the only furniture. They were tense and wary, but when there had been no outcry after a minute had passed, they risked straightening up to look through the windows.

They had a much clearer view now, and could see that the penal settlement was built on somewhat military lines. There was a large open parade ground or exercise yard, while the surrounding cell blocks were built in parallel rows similar to an army barracks. All the rows ran the length of the island, so that the watchtowers at either end provided a clear view between the lines. Half of the open square was shut from their view by a large block of lighted buildings ahead and again a little to their right, but that part which they could see was filled with groups of armed rebels and uniformed convicts lounging around a series of log fires. Many of them sprawled in sleep, but there were enough remaining awake to cause the three watchers a flutter of apprehension.

Shaw said softly. "That lighted block ahead is part of the staff quarters, and there's a corresponding block on the other side of the square. This side includes the Governor's rooms, and I should imagine that that's where the rebel leaders and the political prisoners are holing up. That's probably why the lights are on."

Larren grimaced. "You said Dominguez would probably be in the solitary cells — where are they?"

"To the right," Shaw answered. "There are two main cell blocks flanking each side of the central exercise yard, and at the end of the yard, slap in the middle where it's directly overlooked by the far watchtower, is the solitary block." He paused, and then went on. "Just to fill in the picture there are four more cell blocks to our left. Those are reserved for the political types. The murderers, rapists, and other hardened thugs are in the remainder."

"Charming," Hansen commented dryly. "It's just like home."

Larren remained silent for a moment, studying the mass of men filling the central square, and speculating on their chances if the mob should become alerted. The prospect was not encouraging, and he didn't like the look of some of the hardened characters in convict clothes. Then he said at last.

"You know the way, Andy. We'd best get moving."

Shaw nodded. "Keep close," he said. "We'll have to cross that open gap between here and the staff block, but after that we should be able to keep in the shadow behind cell block A. Fortunately nobody has bothered to switch on the lights that usually illuminate the inside of the palisade."

As he spoke Shaw was feeling his way through the gloom until he found the back door of the guardhouse. He found it unlocked and opened it carefully. For a moment he strained his eyes along the wide gap between the stockade wall and the backs of the grim stone buildings. Nothing moved in the darkness and he turned to nod briefly before crouching low and darting over to the nearest wall. Larren hesitated a moment to ensure that the policeman had not been seen, and then sprinted swiftly in his wake. Hansen waited another minute, and then joined them.

Shaw led the way again along the back of the staff block, halting a yard from the corner where the building ended. There was another gap before they could reach the back of the first of the long cell blocks, but here they had to cross a pool of light thrown from a window that was just around the corner. As they listened they could hear muttered voices in earnest conversation.

Shaw turned his head slightly and his lips moved in a whisper. "That's coming from the Governor's office. We've got to get past."

"Then I guess we've got to do some more belly-dragging," Hansen murmured. "I'll play the lead guy, then if anything goes wrong I can pepper that window with this." He tapped the sten gun lightly.

Larren nodded in agreement, and he and Shaw stayed back as the American lowered himself to the ground. The sound of voices continued to reach Larren's ears, but the words were in Spanish and he found it pointless to listen. His palm was sweating a little where he gripped his gun, and he watched as Hansen circled wide towards the palisade to avoid the area of light, and then turned in again to reach the black gloom by the cell block wall. Hansen was moving smoothly and swiftly, the sten held ahead of him as he wriggled on his stomach. Larren remembered his first impression of the man as a sleepy rattlesnake, and decided that the thought was apt, except that now Hansen was wide awake.

He saw Hansen reach his goal, and then twist round so that he could cover their advance. He waited for a signal, and when Hansen's head nodded briefly he tapped Shaw on the shoulder.

The Police Inspector lost no time in following Hansen's example, and although his movements were clumsier and lacked the American's practised ease, he too circled the pool of light unseen. Hansen nodded again, and Larren flattened himself to the ground to make his own crossing. He made it without difficulty, and would have kept going if Hansen had not fastened one hand on his arm.

The American inclined his head towards the lighted window, which they could now see clearly, and Larren's muscles gave an involuntary start as he recognized two of the men taking part in the conversation inside. One was the lean-faced Lieutenant Delgado who had sold them out, and the other was the hollow-eyed man in the stained jungle green uniform whom he had last seen during his encounter with the voodoo witchdoctor Medianoche.

For a moment Larren stared, wondering what the man was doing here, and then Hansen indicated that they should withdraw. They eased back to join Shaw, and not until they were well out of hearing did Hansen speak.

"I guess you know who that was?"

Larren nodded. "Rafael's rival — Savalas. I've met him, remember?"

"Sure, I was forgetting. But how the heck does he manage to turn up here?"

"Obviously he wants Rafael."

"I'm not that dumb." Hansen sounded nettled. "But how did he know that Rafael would turn up here? He must have arrived when the cons were first released, because there haven't been any other boats."

"Perhaps he's good at guessing," Shaw put in. "I told you when we were in the swamp that this was the only place that we could hope to reach. The other side would know that too if they had traced the two lorries we had to abandon. And as they must have captured a good many prisoners who saw us all at Oparto's camp they would know that the lorries were the ones we used to escape from the battle area."

"It's beginning to make sense," Larren reflected. "It would explain why the rebels acted so much faster than we had expected in visiting the jail, and also why they've hung around afterwards. They would have released the political prisoners eventually anyway, but after tracking us to the swamp they simply decided to act immediately and hope to kill two birds with one stone. Dominguez would be their main concern, and Savalas probably begged a ride to be sure of Rafael."

"It figures," said Hansen grimly. "We've been trying to buck a stacked deck all along the line."

"And we're still up against it," Shaw reminded them. "We can't afford to hang about."

Larren nodded, and all three hurried along the back of the long cell block. They reached the far end and then moved more warily as they rounded the corner. Directly ahead of them was a large wooden building, which Shaw identified as a storehouse. Beyond it, and still inside the palisade rose the four, widely-spaced legs of the watchtower. The machine gun platform was seventeen foot high and commanded a wide view, but it was still unmanned. The large moon face of the spotlight beside the slackly dangling barrel of the gun was dull and only faintly visible in the starlight.

Shaw pointed to their left and said. "That's cell block B. It runs parallel to this one. Beyond that is the solitary block."

Larren nodded acknowledgment and moved cautiously round the end of the stone wall. After fifteen feet he was able to look down the wide lane that separated the two cell blocks. Most of the doors were swinging open and there was an air of desertion. Larren listened a moment, and then decided that the convicts were probably making the most of their brand new freedom by sleeping out in the open square where they had been celebrating.

He crossed the opening to the end of B block and again squashed himself against the wall. He heard the rustle of movement but did not look round as his companions closed up behind him.

The watchtower was in full view now, and he was thankful that the rebels had not bothered to post a guard on that ugly looking machine gun. He surveyed the rest of the ground, and saw that the doors of the storehouse had been torn open. He glanced round at Hansen and the American understood his meaning look.

"I'll check," Hansen murmured, and then he moved silently to ensure that the storehouse was empty.

Larren inched forward with Shaw at his elbow and risked a swift glance round the next corner. Directly opposite this block, across a wider gap than usual, was a solid stone row of bleak cells set in partial isolation. They were guarded by two rebel soldiers armed with the standardized sten guns, and were clearly in view of the mob of men filling the square, which was again visible through the lane between the rows. Larren's face tightened and he drew back and breathed softly to Shaw.

"You were right, Andy. They are in those solitary cells. There would be no need for a guard otherwise."

Shaw said nothing, and they waited in silence until Hansen re-appeared beside them. Larren touched his lips in warning, and held up two fingers to indicate two guards. Hansen understood.

All three retreated out of hearing, and then Hansen said quietly. "The storehouse is clean. The baddies are all on our left flank."

"That's a help," Larren curled his mouth into a glimmering smile as he spoke. "But we're still going to need some kind of diversion before we can tackle those last two guards. If we don't draw that mob out of the square then one of them is sure to spot what's happening."

"Now if that isn't just fine and dandy." Hansen's eyes gleamed satisfaction. "I was hoping we might need a little diversion. I figured out just the thing when I saw fancy-boy Delgado chumming it up with Savalas. I'll just go liven up that party a little while you and Shaw handle this end."

"A worthy suggestion," Larren murmured. "But aren't you forgetting something? If you draw the mob in that direction you'll he luring them between the rest of us and the way out."

Hansen grinned. "I got that figured too. Among other things in that storehouse I just checked is a whole stack of strong planks, stored there for repairing the bridges I guess. Anyway, they're good long planks, long enough to span that gap between the platform of the watchtower and the top of the stockade. I don't see why you can't borrow one and go out the back way, and you'll have that lovely machine gun up there to cover your retreat if you're spotted."

Larren hesitated, for if possible he had wanted to get away without alerting the settlement at all, but after a moment he had to admit that it would be impossible to divert the men in the square and still do that. He said at last.

"What about you?"

Hansen grinned. "If I can't take care of myself at my age I deserve to get blasted anyhow. I'll see you back at the launch."

Larren remembered that Rosemary Keene was waiting with the launch, and felt a moment of doubt. Then it passed as he realized that Hansen would not come this far and then change his mind.

The American would undoubtedly leave Rafael to rot, but there were still Dominguez, Sam and Caroline to be considered. Finally Larren said.

"Okay, Reb. Make it five minutes, then let fly. That'll give me time to get organized."

Hansen grinned again, and then he rested a hand for a moment on Shaw's shoulder. "Take care of this crum for me. I still owe him a sock on the jaw." He raised the sten gun in salute then vanished into the darkness behind them.

Shaw was puzzled. "What did he mean by that?"

"It's some kind of American humour," Larren explained. Then he added seriously. "I'll leave you here while I try to get round the other side of that solitary block. When the fireworks fly I should be in the right position to take the furthest guard. The near one is sure to start towards the ruckus, and that's when you jump out and crack that revolver across his head."

Shaw looked at the sawn-off Colt in his hand. "I can do it. Don't worry."

Larren smiled, and then he too turned away. He circled round the back of the storehouse, running swiftly, and then crouched low as he ducked past the overshadowing watchtower. There was a second storehouse opposite the first, and he again circled around the back, until at last he arrived at the end of the first of the long cell blocks that ran along the far side of the enclosure. He moved inward to the second cell block, and from there he was in an identical position to Shaw fifty yards away, with the solitary cells in between them.

He paused there a moment to regulate his breathing, and then carefully swapped his Smith & Wesson from hand to hand and back again as he dried each sweating palm in turn. Then he risked a brief glanced around the corner.

Again he could see between the rows of cells to the fire-lit square where the mixed forces of convicts and rebels lay in sleeping disorder, but in this line there were no more guards. Larren's grey-green eyes resembled a cat's in the dark, and he dropped low on his stomach and began to squirm silently forward.

He reached the punishment block, and then turned towards the square, moving faster now that he was sheltered by the inky blackness at the foot of the wall. His movements slowed again as he reached the far corner, and now he was only twenty feet away from the nearest fire, and ten from the nearest man.

With utmost caution he turned the corner, still in shadow but no longer in the absolute darkness that had protected him so far. However, the fires were mercifully burning low, and most of the relaxing men had their backs towards him. He dragged his body inch by inch towards the next corner, with every sense alert for any indication that he had been seen or heard. None came, and it was with relief that he reached within a yard of his goal and then sank low and motionless as he waited for Hansen to shatter the peace of the night.

The only sound was the subsiding crackle of one of the fires as the half-burned logs fell slowly inwards, but after a moment Larren was able to pick out the muffled breathing from some of the nearer men. One shrivelled-faced convict rolled in his sleep and his mouth opened in a low snore. Towards the far end of the square a small number of rebel soldiers squatted around their fire half awake, but even they were beginning to doze. Larren could also hear very distinctly the thudding of his own heart, for both his face and his chest were flat to the ground. Then something, most probably an ant, began to crawl inside his trouser leg and make its way up the long slope of his calf, and he felt a maddening desire to scratch.

With an effort he lay still. A minute passed, and he faintly heard each individual second tick past on his wristwatch. A second minute began to tick away, and he thought that surely Hansen must he there by now. And then the night was ripped open by the chattering snarl of a fast-firing sten.

The sound was accompanied by the crash of breaking glass as the window of the governor's office disintegrated before the hail of gunfire, and was echoed by an uproar of shouts and screams. By then every man in the square was tumbling to his feet and there was complete pandemonium as they grabbed for their weapons. Most of them were too bleary-eyed to do more than gawp in the direction of the staff block, and then a group of soldiers began running towards the disturbance. The rest of the mob began to follow or scatter towards the sides of the square.

The time was ripe and Larren rose swiftly to his feet. Every eye in the square was turned away from him towards the confusion, where a fusilade of revolver shots were now retaliating to the angry clatter of the sten, and no one noticed his timed attack. He rounded the corner and rushed the nearest guard who was already moving towards him. The man tried to jerk up his sten, but Larren's fist lashed out and the extra weight of the Smith & Wesson provided a solid sweetness to the crack that marked the impact. The man's eyes went glassy, and he collapsed with what was probably a broken jaw. The second guard shouted and levelled his sten, and then Andy Shaw sprang at his back from the far end of the darkened lane between the cell blocks.

Shaw's leap carried the remaining guard to the ground and they writhed together like tumbling cats. Larren sprinted forwards, hovered above them for a moment, and then struck downwards once as the two men rolled against him. The Smith & Wesson cracked against the guard's skull and then both bodies hit Larren's legs and he toppled into the heap.

However, that single blow had again been effective, and he and Shaw quickly disentangled themselves and scrambled to their feet. Shaw crouched over the unconscious guard and searched him swiftly. Then he looked up with desperate eyes.

"There are no keys."

Larren hurried back to the first guard, sparing a quick glance for the now empty square as he hurriedly rifled the man's pockets. It seemed as though a dozen stens were now blazing away madly towards the staff block, and Hansen was doing a magnificent job. Then Larren found the keys and saw the relief in Shaw's face as he held them up.

The young Inspector kept watch with Hansen's Colt as Larren frantically went through most of the dozen keys on the big steel ring before he found one that opened the first door. He pulled the door back and Caroline Brand cried his name and stumbled forward into his arms.

He pushed her roughly away.

"Not now," he hissed. "We'll have the reunions later."

She recovered herself and nodded, and then she kept to one side as he quickly released Rafael, Dominguez and Sam Friday in succession. Friday was limping badly as he emerged from the gloom of his cell, but his teeth showed white in the shining blackness of his face.

"Man, I thought you was never comin'," he beamed amiably. He looked swiftly around him, and then moved to pick up one of the sten guns that had been dropped by the ambushed guards.

Dominguez still held on to his cell door for support, and he looked very sick and unsteady. His dark glasses had been taken from him and his pale, intellectual face seemed naked without them. He said weakly but clearly.

"Thank you, Mr Larren — and you, Inspector Shaw. You have arrived only just in time, for we were to have been shot at sunrise tomorrow. The rebel leaders held a pantomime court martial soon after we were captured and the verdict was unanimous."

Larren grinned. "We'll accept our medals later. Reb can't keep the whole settlement amused for ever, so right now we've got to hurry. Rafael, give him some help."

For once the dictator of Maraquilla had achieved the communal spirit, and he moved almost eagerly to obey. Dominguez accepted his assistance gratefully, and they shuffled after Larren as he led the way to the watchtower. Caroline was close behind them and Shaw and Friday brought up the rear.

Larren glanced around to make sure that they were still unthreatened, and then rapped instructions to keep going before sprinting over to the storehouse. He pushed inside, and then stopped as he surveyed the pitch blackness. For one horrible moment he thought that Hansen had lied, and that he had blundered badly in not realizing that it would he impossible to see anything in the darkness. And then his faith in the American returned and he decided that the planks he needed must be close to the door where the faint starlight relieved the opening. He explored deftly with his foot and almost immediately kicked into the stack. There was no time to hunt for the longest plank and he simply grabbed the first one that his hands encountered and pulled it out into the open.

In the same moment the inevitable happened and their escape was noticed.

A bawling voice raised the alarm and was immediately echoed, and Larren saw Sam Friday go down on one knee and open up with his captured sten gun into the gap between the two cell blocks that they had just left. Shaw stopped to back him up, his right arm fully extended as he squeezed off shot after shot from Hansen's Colt.

Dominguez, aided by Caroline and Rafael, was still a dozen yards from the foot of the watchtower as the sound of the mob began to swing towards them, and an outburst of bullets came from the direction of the square.

Larren ran towards them, dragging the vital plank with one hand and pulling free the Smith & Wesson with the other. And then he saw Shaw break away and run. The young policeman sprinted for the watchtower, pushing past their three companions and scrambling madly up the ladder. A burst of sten fire sought hungrily for his climbing figure, and then stopped as Friday depressed his trigger again and cut down its author. Shaw kept on going and reached the platform.

There was a howl of frenzy that seemed to fill the air, and Larren felt cold as he realized that the released convicts had recognized the hated police uniform that Shaw was wearing. They reacted like bulls to a matador's cape, forging ahead of their rebel allies as they rushed down the lanes between the cell blocks. And then Shaw reached the machine gun. He squatted behind it and flashed on the dazzling beam of the spotlight to bring the scene starkly and vividly to life. The mass charge faltered as he sighted down the gun barrel, and then he opened fire.

Larren carried on running, passing Friday who still knelt low cuddling his spitting sten gun, and then he reached the foot of the watchtower. Dominguez and the others were already there, pausing for breath, and above them the night was made hideous by the ripping bursts from the machine gun as Shaw continuously switched his aim from lane to lane to hold their combined enemies back.

Larren tucked the plank under his arm and scrambled awkwardly up the ladder. As soon as he could reach he pushed the plank through the trap door opening on to the platform, and then he descended again. He reached down without ceremony and gripped the back of Dominguez's jacket, and with Rafael steadying from behind he helped the injured man to climb and then manhandled him up on to the platform. Rafael came next, and then Larren swung down again to help Caroline Brand. She looked haggard and frightened, and a wave of her dark gold hair had tumbled forward over her face. Her foot missed a rung and for a moment she was held only by the firmness of his arm around her waist. He gave her an encouraging smile as bullets spattered around them, and then she struggled gamely on.

Larren looked back and saw that Sam Friday was now retreating slowly. He yelled to the big negro to join them, and then he hurried up to the platform behind Caroline.

Shaw was still capably operating both the spotlight and the machine gun, while the two Presidents huddled behind him. Larren found his plank again and knelt on the edge of the platform facing the palisade as he carefully thrust it out. He badly wanted to hurry, but he dared not in case he dropped the plank altogether. The job was awkward, but after a moment Rafael crouched beside him to help. Between them they wedged the far end of the plank between the pointed tops of two of the logs forming the palisade. They drew it back slowly until the near end rested on the platform, and Larren was sweating as he realized that they had bridged the ten foot gap with only inches to spare.

He looked at Rafael and said grimly. "You'll go first. We'll need a fit man to catch the others." Rafael nodded. He stood upright, and while Larren crouched to steady the bridge he walked cautiously down the slight slope to the palisade, his arms spread wide to maintain his balance. The plank sagged, and Rafael stopped nervously. He looked round and Larren nodded him on. Slowly Rafael began again, and a moment later he reached the palisade.

He lowered himself carefully between two of the pointed logs, and then swung his body outside. His hands remained visible for a moment as he gripped the points, and then he dropped.

Larren looked at Vicente Dominguez, the man was scared, and unsure of his own failing strength, but he came forward.

Shaw was blazing away again and Larren had to pause a second to make himself heard.

"Take it steady," he said at last. "You've got to go alone, but you can make it."

Dominguez nodded, and stepped out on to the plank. Larren braced himself again to hold it steady, and sighed with relief when San Quito's President reached the palisade a few moments later. Caroline was already waiting, and she moved across lightly and swiftly.

Larren straightened up without waiting to see her drop to safety, and turned to see Sam Friday pulling himself through the hole in the floor. The noise of battle was still raging as Shaw manned the machine gun, and down below swift figures darted in and out of the moving area of blazing light to fire searching bursts with stens or rifles at the fugitives. Larren moved to help the negro who was having trouble with his injured leg, and as he did so there was a sudden crash and the spotlight went out in a shower of bursting glass. Shaw cursed angrily and hammered back with renewed fury.

Larren hurried Friday across their flimsy bridge, and this time the plank sagged alarmingly beneath the negro's massive bulk. Friday wobbled, and his shoulders and arms shifted in frenzied movement as he fought to retain his balance. The plank twisted in Larren's hands and his wrists almost gave way under the strain of holding it steady. Then the negro threw his sten gun forward over the palisade and lunged to grab the pointed tops. He steadied himself, and then pulled his body forward. A moment later he was sitting astride the palisade, and then he was gone.

Larren looked round for Shaw, and the policeman relaxed his grip on the machine gun and shouted.

"Get over after them, Larren. I'll cover your retreat."

Larren hesitated, but someone had to be last and there was no time to change places now. He turned away grimly and left Shaw still firing as he ran lightly across the plank bridge. It moved loosely and almost threw him down now that there was no one to steady it, but a second later he had reached the palisade and hurriedly lowered himself on the outside. He dropped the last six or seven feet and rolled automatically with the fall.

Caroline appeared to help him as he straightened up, and he saw that they were alone on the narrow strip of beach between the settlement and the fork of the river. She said quickly.

"The others are across. Rafael helped

Dominguez and I sent Sam to join them."

"Good girl," Larren praised her warmly. And without any further delay they moved into the dark water and swam across to the far bank. Friday helped them out and they saw the two Presidents behind him.

"What about the copper?" Friday asked anxiously.

"Someone had to stay. He elected himself." Larren's voice was bleak. Then he added hopefully. "He's a capable type. He might catch us up."

He glanced towards the settlement for a moment, where the shattering bursts of the machine gun still dominated the shouting fury of the night, and then he turned to hurry his charges on. There were excited voices approaching them on this side of the river now, and he guessed that the rebels had used the bridge ahead and were either hunting for Hansen, or coming this way to intercept them. The situation was still desperate, and their only course was to circle widely through the fields and along the edge of the jungle, and hope that they could get past the settlement again without being seen. And then hope again that Hansen and Rosemary were waiting for them with the launch.

Larren took the lead, warning his companions into silence now that they had obtained the cover of darkness. They stumbled along behind him, bunching together and cowed by the sounds of the searching rebels. And then Caroline said in a horrified whisper.

"Simon, look."

They stopped to look behind them, and Larren realized for the first time that the watchtower machine gun was silent. The silhouette of the settlement still showed faintly, and beneath the outline of the tower they saw a dim figure that could only be Shaw inching his way across the shaking plank. As they watched a burst of firing sounded all at once from inside the stockade, and the figure on the plank seemed to spin and stagger in mid air. The plank rocked and Shaw toppled from sight.

Caroline said hoarsely. "They — they'll tear him to pieces."

Larren gripped her arm and said harshly.

"He's already dead, Caroline. He was dead when he fell." There was a black and bitter anger in his heart, and then he turned to lead them further away from the settlement. For the second time Andy Shaw had saved all their lives, and this time the young Inspector had paid with his own.

19

The Power of Voodoo

IT took them half an hour to work
their way round to the jetty where
the launch was waiting, and at any
moment Larren expected that the rebel
forces would anticipate their intentions.
The night was full of rushing bodies,
shouted orders and stray gunshots. One
heavy group had gone running past
them along the path that followed the
Black River into the swamp, but most of
the remainder seemed to have clustered
on the bridge where they squabbled
and argued amongst themselves. Larren
realized then that they were leaderless,
and prayed that they would stay that
way for just a little while longer.

He was thankful for the almost
absolute cover of darkness that protected
them as they stumbled along, and for

the fact that the few noises that their blind progress made unavoidable were lost in the general melee. He could hear Dominguez breathing harshly and painfully, and knew that the wounded President was in bad shape. Friday too was dragging his left leg with difficulty as he attempted to keep pace in the rear.

They neared the jetty and Larren softly instructed them to stay back as he approached alone. He still couldn't quite believe that no one had been sharp enough to check the guard on the two launches, and he had to be sure. There was a sudden rustle in the bushes ahead, and the Smith & Wesson jumped to attention in his hand.

"Easy now," Reb Hansen checked him calmly. "You wouldn't shoot an old buddy, would you?"

Larren relaxed and lowered the gun as the tall outline of the American emerged from the gloom. Hansen's left arm was hanging limply at his side and his right hand was clasped to his shoulder.

"I ducked a little too slow," he explained. "But I wiped out Delgado and Savalas, and half of their buddies as well. I think it's left the rest of the bad guys just slightly disorganized."

"Well I'm glad you didn't duck any slower," Larren said with feeling. "Have you checked the boat."

"It's still there, and Rose is worried sick. The sooner she sees us all again the happier she'll be."

Larren smiled, and then turned to call softly to those behind him. They shuffled up quickly and Hansen's face grew sombre as he made a quick count. He said grimly.

"Where's Shaw?"

Quietly Larren told him.

Hansen was silent a moment, then he said bitterly. "That's war I guess. It's always the kids that get it, while no-good crums like you and me live on for ever. It kinda spoils the fun, don't it?"

He didn't wait for an answer but turned sourly away. They still had no time to lose and hurried down to the jetty. The boards rang beneath their feet as they rushed along it, and Larren was aware that all of them were looking apprehensively towards the forbidding outlines of the gunboats in the river mouth.

The launch's engine started as they reached it, and Larren saw Rosemary Keene standing ready at the wheel. As fast as possible he herded his companions aboard, and then drew his knife to slash through the mooring rope. He shouted to Rosemary to get the boat away, and jumped aboard as the gap widened. The boat roared as the red-head opened the throttle, and then surged like a racing greyhound for the open sea.

They passed within twenty yards of the nearest gunboat as their wake lengthened behind them. There were yells and shouts as the launch's engine alerted the crew, and men began rushing to the gunboat's rails. Larren snapped at his companions to lie flat, and then he thrust forward to relieve Rosemary of the wheel, repeating the order and pushing her down. A flurry of wild shots came towards them, most of them missing completely but a few carving splinters from the cabin roof. Sam Friday hugged his sten gun again and took the opportunity of emptying the last few rounds from the magazine as they sped out of range.

The careering launch left the river mouth and Larren swiftly spun the wheel to starboard in order to hug the coastline. The surface of the sea was relatively calm, but he kept the throttle fully open and their speed made the craft buck wildly over every wave. Rosemary struggled up from the deck at his feet, and then moved to help Hansen who was coming up behind them.

Hansen used his good hand to steady himself against the launch's cowling, and Larren saw the wet stains of blood soaking the shoulder of the man's jacket. He said tightly.

"Where now, Larren?"

"We'll hug the coast for a bit," Larren had to bellow above the rush of spray and wind. "Then when I'm sure that we've given those gunboats the slip we'll head out for the States. We should just make the Florida coast."

There was another movement behind them, and then Dominguez said hoarsely. "There is no need for that, Mr Larren. You may keep on going and head for Aparicio." The wound in his side was bleeding again, and his eyes were pale and tired, but very faintly the President of San Quito was smiling. "The British Government has acted to help us," he explained. "We learned from one of our guards who was somewhat talkative that five hundred men of the British Regular Army have been airlifted to San Quito from their stations in British Guiana. They have re-taken the capital, and are holding it while those of my Generals who, like the brave Colonel Oparto, have remained loyal are quelling the revolt in the interior."

It took a moment for the words to sink in, and then Larren began to smile.

"It's about time," he said. "Whitehall have been sitting on their fingers for so long that I was afraid they were permanently stuck."

* * *

Two evenings later Simon Larren strolled slowly along a secluded beach just outside Aparicio, with Caroline Brand pressing snugly against his side. He was wearing a new, light-weight suit of charcoal grey, while she wore a dark gold dress that nearly matched the soft hair that was now brushing his cheek. Her bruised knees were bound with clean white bandages and were still sore, but not too sore, she had confided wickedly, for making love.

That afternoon they had watched Jose Rafael board a plane at the airport for Maraquilla, with Rosemary Keene and his two surviving bodyguards still at his heels. Sam Friday was still limping awkwardly with the help of a stick, in direct defiance to doctor's orders after a bullet had been dug from the fleshy part of his thigh, and Hansen's left arm was supported by a sling. Despite their patched-up appearance the two shadows still looked a formidable pair, and Hansen had already shortened the barrel of a new Colt to make it fit the shoulder holster that now reposed in his airline bag. Larren had watched their plane take off, and the moment it was airborne his job on San Quito was over.

The revolt on the island colony was still continuing in the interior, but the outcome was now certain and the Communist inspired forces were already facing failure. Sir Basil Trafford, on whose responsibility the British troops patrolling Aparicio had been brought in, had proclaimed martial law with Dominguez's approval, and in the city everything was under control. The Governor had been saved from the

Sunday riots that had started the brief but bloody uprising by the fast action of the bulky Police Commissioner Mackenzie. The zealous old Scot had been so certain of impending trouble that he had arranged for a picked squad of his best men to ensure Trafford's protection the moment it was needed. They had assisted the whole staff of Government House to escape outside the city before the advance wave of rebel troops could reach them. Mackenzie had later commented dourly that as it had been impossible to guarantee the safety of Dominguez and his guest in the parade, he had felt obliged to pull at least one chestnut from out of the fire.

Now, as the moonlight made a silver fantasy of the sea, and the low waves frothed peacefully along the beach, Larren could at last feel that the troubles of San Quito were no longer his concern. His only interest was in the woman by his side.

They reached the shadow of a grove

of palms, fifty yards from the sea's edge, and for a moment they paused. Larren turned over the fine white sand with the toe of his shoe and glanced up at the serrated fronds that curved like an awning above them.

"It hardly seems like the same island," he reflected idly.

"Mmmmm, different island — different world."

Her arm tightened around his waist and her thigh pressed warmly against him. She was silent for a while and then turned her face to look up into his eyes. She smiled, and said.

"It's nice, but I think our hotel room is nicer."

"Now you're beginning to sound like the spy who seduced me in London."

She chuckled. "I didn't have to work very hard." She pulled him round to face her and added seriously. "But honestly, Simon, if we had met under any other circumstances. I think that I would still have tried to seduce you. Because you're my kind of man. It can't last, we both know that. Neither of us can afford to let it last. You could have been killed a dozen times over in the last few days, and the next assignment will be just as dangerous. The same applies to me. Neither of us has any right to fall in love. But just for tonight, we can pretend."

Larren held her, and his face lowered to meet her. "Let's start pretending," he said softly. And then his mouth closed on her expectant lips. It was a long and silent kiss, with only the whisper of the palms and the sighing of the sea to disturb them. And when they parted he could feel every beat of her heart against his chest.

She smiled happily and said. "Let's walk back to the hotel now, Simon. I want you to really make love to me."

Larren nodded, kissed her again, and then slipped his arm around her waist as he started to lead her back across the beach. They took two idling steps and then abruptly a whistle shrilled.

The sound drilled through Larren's

nerves like an electric shock, and automatically his body whipped round. His hand dived to his waistband, and too late he remembered that the spring-loaded Smith & Wesson was no longer there. He had stopped wearing it immediately after his bodyguard assignment had finished. Then the first of the rushing figures spilling from the blackness of the palm grove was upon him.

Larren ducked, and jack-knifed the man into a flying somersault over his shoulders. His fist lashed the second of his attackers on the jaw, and the third bowled over backwards as the toe of a shoe drove cruelly into his groin. The night and the beach seemed to swarm with silently charging negroes, and Larren twisted to help Caroline as she screamed his name. Then a blast of dynamite seemed to explode against his head and the shock waves tore through his brain, blotting out all sight and feeling.

Larren recovered consciousness as

a bucket of sea water was dashed viciously into his face. The impact rocked his head and caused a core of pain to pulse through from the back of his skull. He tasted salt and vaguely sensed that his arms were held fast behind him, wrenching his shoulders in their sockets. Another cascade of sea water doused his head and with an effort he blinked his eyes open, shaking his head to get rid of the running streams that all but blinded him.

He saw the deckboards of a boat, and the bare, splay-toed feet of the negroes who stood on either side of him to hold him down. He felt the faint motion of the boat and knew that she was drifting, and then slowly he raised his head. The knife of pain cut through his skull again, but after a moment his vision cleared and he began to understand. For facing him, and still holding the empty bucket, was the brawny mulatto who had led his first capture by the voodoo terrorists who had ordered him to murder Jose Rafael.

Larren winced as he turned his head, knowing what to expect, and saw again the bizarre voodoo mask that concealed the true identity of the man who called himself Doctor Medianoche. The grim figure again wore the horrible regalia of sharks teeth and barracuda jaws, and the two human skulls that dangled from his belt. Fresh paint glistened in garish design on his black, muscular chest.

Larren twisted his head a little further and found Caroline Brand. She too was pinned down on her knees by two grinning negroes who forcibly held her shoulders. Her hands were clasped close to her breast and her eyes were badly scared as she met his gaze. There was nothing that Larren could say or do to reassure her, and he turned his eyes back to meet Medianoche.

"You are a fool, Mr Larren." The voodooist spoke harshly. "You were given your life on the condition that you performed a small service. You ignored your side of the bargain, and that is why you are here now."

Larren said slowly. "It hardly seems to matter now. General Savalas is dead, and your Communist friends have bungled their attempt to grab control of the island. The revolution is over."

"That may be so." The mask inclined slightly in agreement, and the huge horns that crowned the voodoo man's head moved jerkily against the sky. "But it is not our fault that the Communists have failed, despite the help that we were able to give them. And although Communism has in this case lost, the power of the cult of voodoo goes on. Voodoo has existed for many hundreds of years, Mr Larren, originating in the forests of Africa, and journeying to the Caribbean in the holds of the first slave ships that ever reached these islands. It is like any other form of religion, it thrives, it fades, it exults in the open, or it hides in the depths of the jungle, or the shadows of the graveyards — but always it goes on. Nothing can fully stamp out the power of voodoo, and those who defy our commands, must pay our price."

Medianoche had been clenching his right fist, and now with an abrupt movement he threw it open and a handful of dirt spattered in Larren's face.

"Soil," he hissed savagely. "Soil from a freshly filled grave. Can you taste the scent of death in it, Mr Larren?"

Larren spat in revulsion and Medianoche laughed.

"So you do not like the taste of a grave. Well soon you shall have more than a taste. You broke your word to me, Mr Larren, but I never break mine. And my promise to you was death."

Larren stared up into the slits of the mask that hid his enemy's face, and then a movement from the mulatto made him turn his head. He saw that the big half caste was grinning, and that he was again holding the large jagged stone that he used for a ritual execution. There were dark stains on the sharp edges, and Larren remembered with stark clarity every detail that had accompanied the murder of the native constable whom they had kidnapped from the villa Marola.

He looked around slowly, but there was nothing that could stir him with any hope. The sea that encircled them was moonlit, but completely empty, and the coastline of San Quito was no more than a dark blur on the horizon a mile away. Momentarily he looked into the blue eyes of Caroline Brand, and then he faced the voodoo witchdoctor once more.

He said flatly. "What about the woman? You have no cause to kill her."

Medianoche chuckled. "We have no cause to keep her alive."

The mulatto looked expectantly at his master, and calmly the masked Doctor signed to him to go ahead. The mulatto happily raised his crude stone, and in the same moment there came a sharp cracking sound, like the snapping of a brittle stick. The mulatto's body became rigid in mid-movement, and his eyes bulged with pained surprise. A tiny red hole had appeared in the dead centre of his left breast and he swayed unsteadily before he fell.

Medianoche jerked forward, and then twisted round like a stung cat. The little bark was repeated, and the bullet from the second barrel of Caroline's miniature gun took the ghoulishly garbed Doctor neatly in the heart.

For a moment the remaining voodooists could only stand and gape, and even Larren lost vital seconds before his startled brain began to react. Caroline was still held down on her knees, but now the tiny palm gun that normally reposed an inch below her navel was peeking through her fingers where her hands were still clasped in their prayer-like manner to her breasts.

And then the voodoo witchdoctor staggered back a pace, and fell with a sudden splash over the side of the boat.

Larren recovered a matter of seconds before the negroes who held him, and took swift advantage of their shocked bewilderment.

He hurled himself forward, twisting from their grasp and then rolling on to his back. The quickest of the two men lunged to restrain him, but Larren's foot lashed out and the man reeled back to knock into his companion. In the confusion that followed Larren reached inside his jacket for the hidden knife that never left him, and changed it deftly from his left hand to his right as he scrambled to his feet.

He faced three men now, for one of Caroline's guards was struggling with her savagely as he attempted to wrest the empty gun from her fingers. The three rushed in close formation, but Simon Larren with a knife in his hand was the most lethal fighting machine that homo sapiens had ever produced.

The blade flashed in the moonlight as Larren leapt to one side, and the first negro doubled forward, screeching suddenly as he clutched at his stomach. Larren ducked on one knee to avoid a clumsy blow, and the stained blade thrust again and bit home. The third man yelled with terror and turned to leap for safety over the side of the boat.

Larren straightened up as the splash of spray came inboard and then moved to help Caroline. The fourth negro saw him coming and realized that he was alone. The man's eye's bulged fearfully, and then he too dived desperately into the sea.

Caroline sprawled on the deck of the boat, and Larren knelt beside her. She was sobbing for breath and her body shuddered with relief as her arms locked around him. He held her close, lowering his knife and soothing her with caresses and words. The only sounds were the slapping of the sea against the boat's hull, and the splashing of the last two voodooists as they swam frantically for the shore.

Larren kissed Caroline's tear-stained

face and said softly. "Easy — easy now. It's all over." He smiled and added. "You did a marvellous job. I had completely forgotten that you had that little pistol tucked away."

She trembled against him, and then said weakly. "I got it out on the beach while they were waiting for the boat. You were unconscious and they just threw me down beside you. There were too many of them then for just two bullets to do any good, and so I pushed it down the front of my dress and waited. Most of them had to be left behind when the boat did come, but I still had to wait for you to recover to back me up."

"You were marvellous," Larren repeated, as he helped her to her feet. She stood against him unsteadily and then looked round.

"What — what happened to the witchdoctor?"

"Your shot knocked him over the side."

She stared at the darkened sea for

a moment, but there was no sign of the bizarre voodoo mask or its evil wearer.

She said at last. "So we'll never know who he was."

Larren shrugged. "It doesn't really matter. He was Doctor Medianoche — Doctor Midnight — I'd never be able to think of him as anyone else. By now he's barracuda meat, and I'm happy enough just knowing that."

She looked down for a moment at the three bodies, the mulatto and the two negroes, that still littered the boat's deck, and then Larren turned her away.

"I think it really is all over now," he said softly. "And we've already paid for our hotel room in Aparicio."

20

Report from Maraquilla

LONDON'S streets were damp and glistening, and the September sun was squinting through the last drops of a brisk rain storm as Simon Larren parked his white MG sports car near St. James Park and decided to walk the rest of the way to Whitehall. Ten minutes later he was being passed into the familiar book-lined office by a smart young secretary in her twenties. The girl's face was new, but it was attractive and there was a figure to match. She had dark hair and a ready smile, and she looked at him with interest. Larren recalled that the previous secretary had been due for a holiday, and guessed that this was a replacement. He smiled back at her and then Smith spoke.

"Come in, Larren. It's nice to see you back."

Regretfully Larren closed the door behind him and turned his attention to the paunchy little man behind the desk. As always Smith looked like the model picture of an average nine-to-six commuter, and as unassuming as his name. There was a black bowler hat and a rolled umbrella hanging from the hat-stand, and Larren doubted if even he could have picked out his employer from the millions on the rush hour trains.

"Sit down," the little man said. "I have a report here that might interest you." Larren sat down and Smith watched him carefully as he added. "It concerns Maraquilla."

Larren looked across the desk, and for a moment their eyes met. There was a pause of silence, but quite suddenly Larren knew exactly what was in that report, and he knew that Smith had expected him to know.

The little man said bluntly. "Things

have been happening in Maraquilla. Six hours ago President Jose Rafael was found shot dead in the bedroom of his luxury palace in the country's capital. He had been shot through the heart with a bullet from a Colt 45. One of his bodyguards found him — the negro — Sam Friday. Curiously though, the other man — Hansen — has vanished, and it appears that he's taken Rafael's red-headed mistress with him."

Smith paused, and his grey eyes searched Larren's face again. He clasped his hands before him on the desk and asked.

"Didn't you tell me that this man Hansen always favoured a Colt 45?"

Larren's face was blank. "As a matter of fact, he did." He paused and then added wryly. "This is somewhat disappointing, after all the trouble I took to keep Rafael alive."

Smith was silent, and unconvinced.

Larren met the grey eyes blandly, and then asked.

"Who controls Maraquilla now?"

"A relatively new man, a rather obscure doctor of philosophy named Garcia. It seems that he has the backing of a large group of reformists, and that most of the country has swung solidly behind him. He's already announced new measures to increase the standard of living, and on the face of it it sounds like a new and better deal for Maraquilla."

Smith gazed at his agent for a moment longer, and then he relaxed. He dismissed the subject and said briskly.

"No doubt you've read that Vicente Dominguez is fit and on his feet again. San Quito is settling back to normal and Sir Basil Trafford feels secure enough to release the troops we sent him. There is one thing that hasn't reached the papers yet that might interest you. And that is that Police Inspector Andrew Shaw has been awarded a posthumous George Cross."

Larren said quietly. "He earned it."

Smith nodded. "No doubt he did. Perhaps you earned one too, but of course we've had to hush up the fact that you were even there."

"Of course," Larren said dryly. Then he glanced across the desk again. "But you haven't mentioned Caroline Brand, I haven't seen her since we returned to London."

Smith smiled. "Miss Brand is fit and well. But unfortunately a little job cropped up in Budapest, and among her many other — er — talents, Miss Brand speaks fluent Hungarian."

It was Smith's turn to act blankly as Larren gave him a hard look. And then Larren realized that the little man was right, and that there was no future in their both remaining in London. It was best that they were parted. He felt resentment for a moment, and then it died and an imp of temptation began to whisper in its place. The imp grew and Larren slowly began to smile. He leaned forward confidentially and said.

"Just in case you're considering a

replacement to finish her original mission, I'll let you into a secret. I rather fancy that sexy little secretary you've got outside."

THE END

A FOOT IN THE GRAVE
Bruce Marshall

About to be imprisoned and tortured in Buenos Aires, John Smith escapes, only to become involved in an aeroplane hijacking.

DEAD TROUBLE
Martin Carroll

Trespassing brought Jennifer Denning more than she bargained for. She was totally unprepared for the violence which was to lie in her path.

HOURS TO KILL
Ursula Curtiss

Margaret went to New Mexico to look after her sick sister's rented house and felt a sharp edge of fear when the absent landlady arrived.

THE DEATH OF ABBE DIDIER
Richard Grayson

Inspector Gautier of the Sûreté investigates three crimes which are strangely connected.

NIGHTMARE TIME
Hugh Pentecost

Have the missing major and his wife met with foul play somewhere in the Beaumont Hotel, or is their disappearance a carefully planned step in an act of treason?

BLOOD WILL OUT
Margaret Carr

Why was the manor house so oddly familiar to Elinor Howard? Who would have guessed that a Sunday School outing could lead to murder?

THE DRACULA MURDERS
Philip Daniels

The Horror Ball was interrupted by a spectral figure who warned the merrymakers they were tampering with the unknown.

THE LADIES OF LAMBTON GREEN
Liza Shepherd

Why did murdered Robin Colquhoun's picture pose such a threat to the ladies of Lambton Green?

CARNABY AND THE GAOLBREAKERS
Peter N. Walker

Detective Sergeant James Aloysius Carnaby-King is sent to prison as bait. When he joins in an escape he is thrown headfirst into a vicious murder hunt.

MUD IN HIS EYE
Gerald Hammond

The harbourmaster's body is found mangled beneath Major Smyle's yacht. What is the sinister significance of the illicit oysters?

THE SCAVENGERS
Bill Knox

Among the masses of struggling fish in the *Tecta*'s nets was a larger, darker, ominously motionless form . . . the body of a skin diver.

DEATH IN ARCADY
Stella Phillips

Detective Inspector Matthew Furnival works unofficially with the local police when a brutal murder takes place in a caravan camp.

STORM CENTRE
Douglas Clark

Detective Chief Superintendent Masters, temporarily lecturing in a police staff college, finds there's more to the job than a few weeks relaxation in a rural setting.

THE MANUSCRIPT MURDERS
Roy Harley Lewis

Antiquarian bookseller Matthew Coll, acquires a rare 16th century manuscript. But when the Dutch professor who had discovered the journal is murdered, Coll begins to doubt its authenticity.

SHARENDEL
Margaret Carr

Ruth didn't want all that money. And she didn't want Aunt Cass to die. But at Sharendel things looked different. She began to wonder if she had a split personality.

MURDER TO BURN
Laurie Mantell

Sergeants Steven Arrow and Lance Brendon, of the New Zealand police force, come upon a woman's body in the water. When the dead woman is identified they begin to realise that they are investigating a complex fraud.

YOU CAN HELP ME
Maisie Birmingham

Whilst running the Citizens' Advice Bureau, Kate Weatherley is attacked with no apparent motive. Then the body of one of her clients is found in her room.

DAGGERS DRAWN
Margaret Carr

Stacey Manston was the kind of girl who could take most things in her stride, but three murders were something different . . .

THE MONTMARTRE MURDERS
Richard Grayson

Inspector Gautier of Sûreté investigates the disappearance of artist Théo, the heir to a fortune.

GRIZZLY TRAIL
Gwen Moffat

Miss Pink, alone in the Rockies, helps in a search for missing hikers, solves two cruel murders and has the most terrifying experience of her life when she meets a grizzly bear!

BLINDMAN'S BLUFF
Margaret Carr

Kate Deverill had considered suicide. It was one way out — and preferable to being murdered.

BEGOTTEN MURDER
Martin Carroll

When Susan Phillips joined her aunt on a voyage of 12,000 miles from her home in Melbourne, she little knew their arrival would germinate the seeds of murder planted long ago.

WHO'S THE TARGET?
Margaret Carr

Three people whom Abby could identify as her parents' murderers wanted her dead, but she decided that maybe Jason could have been the target.

THE LOOSE SCREW
Gerald Hammond

After a motor smash, Beau Pepys and his cousin Jacqueline, her fiancé and dotty mother, suspect that someone had prearranged the death of their friend. But who, and why?

CASE WITH THREE HUSBANDS
Margaret Erskine

Was it a ghost of one of Rose Bonner's late husbands that gave her old Aunt Agatha such a terrible shock and then murdered her in her bed?

THE END OF THE RUNNING
Alan Evans

Lang continued to push the men and children on and on. Behind them were the men who were hunting them down, waiting for the first signs of exhaustion before they pounced.

CARNABY AND THE HIJACKERS
Peter N. Walker

When Commander Pigeon assigns Detective Sergeant Carnaby-King to prevent a raid on a bullion-carrying passenger train, he knows that there are traitors in high positions.

TREAD WARILY AT MIDNIGHT
Margaret Carr

If Joanna Morse hadn't been so hasty she wouldn't have been involved in the accident.

TOO BEAUTIFUL TO DIE
Martin Carroll

There was a grave in the churchyard to prove Elizabeth Weston was dead. Alive, she presented a problem. Dead, she could be forgotten. Then, in the eighth year of her death she came back. She was beautiful, but she had to die.

IN COLD PURSUIT
Ursula Curtiss

In Mexico, Mary and her cousin Jenny each encounter strange men, but neither of them realises that one of these men is obsessed with revenge and murder. But which one?

LITTLE DROPS OF BLOOD
Bill Knox

It might have been just another unfortunate road accident but a few little drops of blood pointed to murder.

GOSSIP TO THE GRAVE
Jonathan Burke

Jenny Clark invented Simon Sherborne because her daily gossip column was getting dull. Then Simon appeared at a party — in the flesh! And Jenny finds herself involved in murder.

HARRIET FAREWELL
Margaret Erskine

Wealthy Theodore Buckler had planned a magnificent Guy Fawkes Day celebration. He hadn't planned on murder.

SANCTUARY ISLE
Bill Knox

Chief Detective Inspector Colin Thane and Detective Inspector Phil Moss are sent to a bird sanctuary off the coast of Argyll to investigate the murder of the warden.

THE SNOW ON THE BEN
Ian Stuart

Although on holiday in the Highlands, Chief Inspector Hamish MacLeod begins an investigation when a pistol shot shatters the quiet of his solitary morning walk.

HARD CONTRACT
Basil Copper

Private detective Mike Farraday is hired to obtain settlement of a debt from Minsky. But Minsky is killed before Mike can get to him. A spate of murders follows.